GENIUS

GENIUS

A Novel

THOMAS RAYFIEL

TriQuarterly Books
Northwestern University Press
Evanston, Illinois

TriQuarterly Books
Northwestern University Press
www.nupress.northwestern.edu

Copyright © 2016 by Thomas Rayfiel. Published 2016 by TriQuarterly
Books / Northwestern University Press. All rights reserved.

Printed in the United States of America

10 9 8 7 6 5 4 3 2 1

Library of Congress Cataloging-in-Publication Data
    Rayfiel, Thomas, 1958– author.
Genius : a novel / Thomas Rayfiel.
    pages cm.
    ISBN 978-0-8101-3246-7 (pbk. : alk. paper)—ISBN 978-0-8101-3247-4
    (ebook)
1. Genius—Fiction. 2. Small cities—Social conditions—Fiction. 3. Cancer—
Patients—Fiction. I. Title.
    PS3568.A9257G46 2016
    813.54—dc23
                                                          2015029688

for Claire

It would detain us too long here to trace the steps whereby a man's *genius*, from being an invisible, personal, and external attendant, became his true self, and then his cast of mind, and finally (among the Romantics) his literary or artistic gifts. To understand this process fully would be to grasp that great movement of internalization, and that consequent aggrandizement of man and desiccation of the outer universe, in which the psychological history of the West has so largely consisted.

—C. S. Lewis, *The Discarded Image*

GENIUS

CHAPTER ONE

In Saint Louis, we are accosted.

"Five years ago, I looked just like you."

It is a lady. It is always a lady. This one is old—forty, at least—with an enormous bag. She looms over us, reluctant but determined, testifying at a revival meeting.

"And now I'm cancer free!"

"Thank you," Mother smiles, figuring that will do.

But no. The woman leans close. I can smell her perfume. Luckily, I am still on anti-vomit medication.

"Jesus loves you," she whispers, and then takes off, like she has set the timer on a bomb.

"Well, wasn't that nice?"

"You think that means in five years I'll look just like her?"

We watch the meddlesome do-gooder waddle her way to the next gate.

"You know, Kara, when someone tries to help, the least you can do is be civil."

"She wasn't trying to help. She wasn't even talking to me."

"Yes, she was. She—"

"Jesus loves *you*," I explain.

I do not know what that means. Lately, I have been saying whatever comes into my head. Nobody questions me. Ever since my diagnosis they tippy-toe all around, act like I have access to secret wisdom, inside information. But I do not. That is the joke. It is summer, and all I have is stage 3 non-Hodgkin's lymphoma.

Our connecting flight is delayed. By the time we reach Little Rock it is late afternoon. Mother's car is the same as ever, a nest of worn seat covers, crumpled candy bar wrappers, and discarded circulars that are molded to her shape, that have formed *around* her.

. . . as have I? I wonder, fitting snugly in the passenger side.

We get off Route 10 and head into the setting sun. I am blinded. She is not. She does not even have dark glasses on.

"Have you given any more thought to what we talked about?"

She has not mentioned it since last night, but now that we are almost home I can tell it has been on her mind the whole time.

"It's fine in a place like Brooklyn," she continues. "I saw plenty of girls there who could have benefited from being bald, considering how they treated the hair they were blessed with. But here, if you don't at least wear a hat . . ."

I cannot see, I realize, because I do not have eyebrows. I blink furiously, nibble away at the rays, taking in town one tiny bite at a time.

"If I 'don't at least wear a hat,' then what?"

"People will talk."

"I never knew people here to talk. Not about anything of consequence."

The GTO is out front. He leaves it by the curb so she will not park him in. She has a tendency to do that. By accident. "Oh, do you really want to go out tonight, Gerald? Then I'd have to move the car."

I open the door and push against the seat. Nothing happens.

She is getting our luggage out of the trunk. We threw tons of stuff away, gave as much as we could to my roommates, but in the end there were still the same two fat suitcases I had arrived with, full up. I do not understand. I thought I had gotten rid of everything.

I push again.

Her knees appear at eye level.

"Just give me a minute."

"I'll get Gerald."

She clacks off. Heels on crumbling asphalt.

The suitcases, I think.

I lean out, brace against one—it weighs more than I do—and take my first breath of hot, muddy air. The light, no matter what direction I face, has figured it can penetrate my vision at will. Eyebrows, eyelashes, I thought they were just an excuse to waste money on cosmetics. Who knew they kept out . . . whatever is electrocuting my brain? I smear a few tears, like splashing water on my face. By the time Gerald arrives, I can smile.

"Well, look at you," he says.

"No hugs," Mother warns.

He wraps me up in a big one.

"Get her away from me," I whisper, "before I kill her."

At the kitchen table, I lower myself into a chair. Mother makes a fuss about having Gerald bring the suitcases upstairs. I listen as he puts them in my old room, which he moved into after I left. Now, apparently, he has moved out again.

"You didn't have to do that!" I call.

She is giving him a nonstop litany of whispered instructions, warnings, forbiddings, and demands, none of which, I know from experience, he is paying the slightest attention to. I look at the fronts of cabinets and drawers, filling in what is behind each. I have not been away long enough to forget, that is the problem. Not been away long enough to see old things as new.

"You didn't have to move out," I tell Gerald, when they return.

He shrugs.

Either he has grown more muscles or more fat, it is hard to say which. With curly blonde hair and a wedge of belly showing above tight jeans, he is a grinning teddy bear come to life. Next to Mother though, with her tiny, perfectly assembled look, the "trim" figure of which she is so proud, maybe he has got a little stuffing coming out, maybe one of those shiny button-eyes is loose.

"Everything is exactly as you left it," she says.

"But I didn't leave it like anything. I cleared it out for Gerald."

"Like it was before, I mean."

"—don't sleep here much anyway."

"Well, that's not true. I have to wake you every morning before I go to work. And Sundays, he snores so loud—"

"How's Delilah?"

He frowns. Am I that far behind? I have made it a point, over the years, to follow Gerald's love life. It has proved more fun than having one of my own.

"She keeps good company," he allows.

"Not with you?"

He shrugs again. They are beyond him, his romances. They blow over him like weather. He just makes the best of it. Also, he likes to shrug. I have caught him, when he leaves the bathroom door open after a shower, admiring his shoulders in the mirror, turning them this way and that.

"Delilah Samson is a very persistent girl," Mother sighs.

"You look like you could use a nap."

"Just let her rest a bit, Gerald."

"Can you make it up the stairs?" he asks.

"Of course I can."

"Oh, I forgot," she says abruptly, and goes off, nattering about an extra blanket. Her head is at a strange angle, as if she is examining the baseboard that runs along the hall.

I look down and see I am shivering.

"I could help."

"How?"

"Help you get to your room."

"I can make it just fine, thanks."

But I cannot. My fingers get waylaid by the banister. I always loved the big knob at the bottom where the dark maple whorls in on itself. Most of the house is rundown and plain. It was gutted some time in the past and made modern in a particularly ugly way. This is one of the few original details left. As a child, I made a ritual of running my hand over the knob, caressing it like an amulet. I still do. Except now the rest of me hangs off the softened wood, deadweight.

Mother is hiding her face in the linen closet, talking about cold nights.

"Quick," I whisper.

He scoops me up. For a little brother, he is big. I am alarmed, though, at how easily he cradles me in his arms. He does not grunt or sigh, does not tilt backward as he carries me up the stairs. I weigh less than a bag of potato chips.

"So, no Delilah?"

"She's around."

"Well, if she's just around, then who's front and center these days?"

"What do you mean?"

"Who's making goo-goo eyes at you now?"

"—big city has certainly made you more direct," he says, dumping me gently on the bed.

Twenty-three years of accumulated memory dust flies up.

"I don't want to kick you out of your room, Gerald."

"It's OK. It gave her something to do."

He motions to the walls, desk, and dresser, all of which, I see now, have been *restored*, as if she is the curator of a natural history museum. Posters I know for a fact got faded and thrown away are magically fresh, tacked up at perfect right angles, as they never were in real life. There is a rainbow decal on the window that I had in fifth grade. It peeled off one day. Now it is back. Who remembers such things? By the pillows is a doll that resided for years in the attic. Raggedy Ann. It is my room, all right, but not exactly as I left it, more a compilation, a Greatest Hits album. I squint and see different periods of my childhood come in and out of focus. It is a room to die in.

I nod at the dresser.

"I don't suppose she managed to recreate my stash at the back of the sock drawer."

"I left you a little something."

He looks at his phone.

"Party?"

"Not exactly."

"Go."

"It's your first night back."

"Not my last, though. Besides, I'm tired."

"She's not so terrible, you know."

I raise my eyebrows. Well, I would raise my eyebrows, if I had any. Probably I get all bug-eyed. Warmth floods me. I have been strenuously, resolutely, not-looking at myself, the past few weeks. You would be shocked at how many reflective surfaces there are to avoid in this world, other people's expressions being the worst. In them, I glimpse a shorn scalp and pale, mug-shot face stunned by happenstance. No one you would ever want to meet. Only now, thawed by my brother's welcoming gaze, do I find an acceptable Me.

"You like the room?" she asks, returning with a quilt that smells of camphor.

"It's great, Ma. Thanks."

"Of course I didn't presume to buy you new clothes."

"I'll unpack later."

"Except in the foundation department."

"The what?"

She pulls open the top drawer and a mountain of snowy white bras springs to life.

"We can't have you going in two different directions at the same time."

"I think I'm going to throw up."

"I'll get a bucket."

It comes that way, unexpected and complete, a hand, a giant rubber-gloved hand, wringing me out, squeezing me dry.

"I've only got this," she panics, coming back with a flowery ceramic bowl. "Maybe it would be better if you—"

I grab it just before letting loose. A cup of tea I had when we landed, then half-digested airport food, and finally the tarry indefinable essence-of-who-I-am, or was, that the spasms wrench out one grotesque morsel at a time. The last of the city, I mourn, clutching the bowl, making hideous barking sounds.

When I look, she is slumped against the door frame. Her makeup has fallen off her face. She teeters on unsteady heels, a small woman, watching her firstborn, not knowing what to do.

Bluebelle Road is in a perfectly acceptable part of town, not where the big houses are, up on the ridge, but not down by the creek either. It is mostly an exercise in geometry, or so it appears from the roof outside my window, pavement narrowing in the distance, lawns, despite personal touches, helplessly conforming to the pattern they were created to represent. The people too, when they climb out of their cars and slog to the front door, resemble soft, squashy creatures forced into glass containers, their eyes and hands and bellies pressed up against a barrier they cannot see or even—except in flashes of horrified awareness—sense. I take another deep hit. I have not smoked since the last time I was here. I never smoke in New York. There is no need. I gauge the distance between the edge of this tiny outcropping and the familiar cracks in the cement walkway below. Not nearly enough height to commit suicide from. I would hardly break a bone.

Normally, this is the hour when I work. I am a night person. I have brought a whole folder of notes with me, preliminary research for my dissertation. But the prospect of reading them over does not appeal. The gears of my mind spin free with no corresponding teeth to engage them.

What did I do at 1:45 a.m. when I "lived" here? Plot, very carefully, how to get away. Perfect grades. Full scholarship. But even more important than the positives were the lists I made of what not to do. Because they are what trip you up. I have seen so many people fail in their dreams because what they wanted turned out to be *flawed* from the outset, just the same old mistakes in disguise. So I hardened myself against the obvious errors: sexual attraction, family affection, self-doubt . . . Self-doubt actually constitutes the chief pitfall. It is what leads to the others, throwing yourself before the onrushing train of love or letting cheap sentimentality supply arguments for not turning your back on home. I swore never to question, never to be wracked by guilt.

Yet these prohibitions, which I endlessly repeated to strengthen my resolve, I now find smooth and worn as sea stones. They have outlived their utility. Yes, I got away. And here I am, back again. So what? More importantly, what is Christy Lee doing at this moment? By 1:45, she used to be in the process of unfurling like a night-flower, but not to sit at a desk and follow the reasoning of, say,

Gottfried Wilhelm Leibniz. No, she would be stretching her arms high overhead, itching for action.

Leibniz proposed seeing the mind as a mill, an unmanned factory. I feel mine, long mothballed by chemo, by radiation, but, even before then, by prolonged intellectual exertion (is that possible? can keeping your head down and focusing be yet another form of sloth?), creak tentatively to life.

"How come you're dressed like that?"

Here, everyone acts as if physical appearance is a team effort. When you fail to obey the rules, you are letting the side down.

"Dressed like what?"

"Is that a coat?"

"Of course it's a coat. It's super lightweight. Feel."

She very warily, like it might be sticky, reaches out and squeezes my arm through the sleeve.

"You are skin and bones, girl."

"That's why I need the coat."

"I like your head."

"I knew you would."

Christy was the onrushing train of love and I just let her pass, roar right through the whistle-stop of my heart, hooting away, whipping up tornadoes of trash. What I felt was not worth her slowing down for. But she knew I was there. She is not stupid, which, for most ordeals life presents you with, is far more useful than being smart.

I must look like a transplanted famine victim, naked head lolling atop a tightly zipped winter jacket, bare feet sticking out of skinny jeans that still manage to sag.

We are sitting on the porch. Martin, her husband, was asleep when I got here. She was in the front room, watching TV. I admit, I spied. I wanted to look for signs of age. She tends to dazzle when she faces me straight on. I peered through the glass and zeroed in

11

on that telltale patch under her chin, looking for an accumulation of flesh, or its opposite, the red strain of tension. But there was none. She was still Christy L., the girl too cool to be head cheerleader. The girl I once went swimming with in the woods, who burned ticks off me with a glowing cigarette and did not leave a single mark. About the only difference from high school is what she is drinking.

"You on the wagon?" she asks, pouring herself another glass from the tall pitcher she brought out.

"It's contraindicated for my medication. What is that, anyway?"

"Long Island Iced Tea," she pronounces carefully, stirs it once, and licks her finger. "Wherever that is."

"That's where I live. I mean geographically. Brooklyn is at the end of Long Island."

"Well, then you live at the end of my drink."

She toasts me.

"Can I see him?"

"He's asleep."

"But can't we just go in?"

She gives me a long, examining stare.

I once let slip, to Mother, how perfect I thought Christy looked. "Perfect?" she snorted. "Perfect like a fetus." That shocked me. I had never heard that word cross her lips before. I knew what she meant, though. Christy had the most unblemished skin and the most regular features. We did not just want to look like her, we wanted to *be* her. I wonder how she put up with it. I knew there was another Christy underneath, or rather the only Christy, because the rest was just people's notions. The question that used to torture me was: did she know that there was someone else there, independent of the girl with the perfect face, the perfect exercise book handwriting, who now signs her letters *Christine Casimir*?

"He cries a lot."

"You breast-feed?"

"Hell no."

"And how's Martin?"

"Busy."

She pronounces that with a kind of neutrality, as if she has not decided if it is good or bad.

I do notice one sign of age. When she drains her glass, she wriggles, like she is trying to get into a mood, fit into old clothes. Before, she would take a sip of beer and forget all about it, tap ash into the can a minute later.

"We haven't bonded yet."

"You and Sheldon?"

"Shelby."

"I'm sorry. Shelby. What kind of name is that, anyway? Some relative of Martin's?"

"He was a general, honey."

"Oh. Of course."

Martin is a Civil War buff. He plays with toy soldiers. The first few times Christy mentioned him in her letters that is all she said. "He plays with toy soldiers." I began to think it was some kind of euphemism, maybe having to do with masturbation. But then, after the marriage, I saw their basement and understood. He plays with toy soldiers.

"I mean, I love Shel," she sighs, "but sometimes it's like he's looking right through me."

"Could that be physical? I don't think they have much depth perception, at this age."

She regards me with superior knowledge, whether that of a mother or just an attractive woman I cannot say. She is sprawled back in the glider, dictating the rhythm we sway to.

"How long are you here for?"

"Just a couple of weeks."

"That's not what your mother thinks."

"I lost my sublet. She acts like it was the only apartment left in New York City."

"And you got another year of school?"

"Two."

"Then what?"

"Then you have to call me Doctor."

"Being sick's not going to get in the way?"

"No."

"Your mother is under the impression that—"

"My mother is a fool!" I snap, with a vehemence that surprises even me. "She doesn't . . ."

I pat my pockets, hoping to find the remnants of Gerald's gift, before remembering I left the rest of the joint at home.

". . . doesn't what?"

"She doesn't even take it serious. She acts like it's some comeuppance I got for moving up North or thinking I was smarter than everyone else or for refusing to shave my legs. She thinks if I just backtrack to wherever it was that I took this wrong turn in the road, then everything will be fine, everything will go back to being *normal*."

I slump against the wood of the glider, exhausted.

"I'm sure she's just looking out for you, Kara. Like always."

"Can we see Shelby now?"

"All right," she grumbles. "I must say, I wouldn't have thought you'd turn out to be just another baby whore. Worse than Ilene. She waltzes in without knocking and goes right upstairs. Doesn't even give me the time of day."

Ilene is her mother-in-law. Her "mother-in-slaw," Christy calls her, still a little put off by Martin's Polish heritage. So that is the problem, I note, as we creep up the carpeted stairs. She is jealous of all the attention. I would have thought it might be a relief, having people's eyes slide over you, for a change. But I guess you come to expect it.

"Do. Not. Wake. Him." she orders sternly, ice tinkling, and pushes open the door.

There is a night-light, providing enough illumination to show a nursery out of a magazine. The wallpaper has elephants, monkeys, giraffes; no carnivores, I notice idly. From deep at the bottom of a miniaturized prison cell comes the sound of breathing. A mobile hangs over the top. The room smells of talcum powder and something else.

"I should empty the diaper pail more often," she whispers.

I am surprisingly moved. His head, sticking out from the blanket, is translucent. I can see his brain, pure, unsullied, ready to take on the world.

"It is the grossest thing," she goes on. "Ilene fed him boiled lima beans once, without asking my permission, of course, and they came right through him, intact. Makes you think that we're just these *processors*, you know. Like worms. That that's the only reason we're here, to convert everything back to waste."

I am overcome, maybe because he is bald, like me.

"Can I pick him up?"

"No, you may not. He'll cry for hours."

"Doesn't he have some kind of feeding around now?"

"I'll spare you that," she says dryly. "Especially the part where he barfs up all over my shoulder. Come on out, honey. You're . . ."

She leads me, firmly, back into the hall.

". . . looking a little vulnerable in there."

"I just wanted to hold him."

"Don't go all baby-crazy on me. I can't handle one more person acting emotionally retarded because I pumped out another Casimir."

We are on the landing that runs along the top floor. It is a very well-appointed house. Nothing creaks. The ideal setting for Scarlett O'Hara histrionics, but that is not Christy's style.

"You'll love him," I assure her.

15

"That's what I'm afraid of. Once I love him it's like the trap has sprung shut. Then I'll have to gnaw off my foot." She smiles. "C'mon. I'll show you something else."

We tiptoe, two giggling cat burglars, down the hall to the master bedroom.

"I can't go in there."

"Sure you can. I do. Every night."

She slips her arm around my waist and guides me into the heavy-curtained gloom. There is no light, but she is so certain of her power, the way she can make my legs move in sync with hers, that we arrive, without crashing, at a thick leather armchair by what is obviously the bed.

"He wears earphones," she says in a normal speaking voice. "Very expensive. They cancel out everything."

My eyes, adjusting, make out a long rumpled lump on one side of the king-size mattress.

"Oh, that's sweet."

"What is?"

"How he left a space for you."

"You want to lie there?"

"No."

"But you want to hold my child."

"That's different."

"See, to me they're two parts of the same story."

We are wedged together in the chair. A roll of leather pushes against my side, while her hip butts against the other. Her hand is still around my waist. Now her fingers lazily flirt with the top button of my jeans.

"Don't get me wrong. I love him."

"Martin?" I ask uncertainly.

"He's a good guy."

"He always was."

"Although I can't say I noticed him much, growing up."

"Well, he was too rich."

I cannot move. I am imprisoned. But even if I could, it would only seem like an invitation for her to continue what she is doing. A response.

"I keep seeing those lima beans," she sighs.

"How's the sex?"

"The sex is fucking fantastic. It's fantastic fucking. I have no complaints."

"You never do. Complain, I mean. Not to anyone but me."

"Is this—?" She pauses, shifting so she can reach down. She is exploring, caressing, teasing. "Is this contraindicated for your medication?"

My silence is the answer she is used to getting. When we first started hanging out together, she said, "You talk so much in class, but with me you can be awfully quiet." And I, of course, said nothing.

"I know I'll fall in love with Shelby," she resumes. "I'm easy. I always was. Weak."

"You're not weak," I manage to get out.

"I am in that department. Not like you. You're far more well defended."

"I never thought of myself that way."

"Oh yes. You are one tough nut to crack."

"I think he's waking up."

"He's just having a dream."

Aren't we all? I reflect.

"I'm glad you came back when you did. See, this is a real in-between time for me. Before I take the plunge."

"Wasn't getting married taking the plunge?"

"No. That was more like going in up to your knees. I mean, I could always take back anything I said or felt. At least that's how it seemed."

"What about—?"

"Hey babe!" she calls. Martin's eyes are open now. "Look who's here!"

CHAPTER TWO

"I am so sorry," Vallomthail says.

"Don't be."

"Who was that woman?"

"My mother."

"She seemed very reluctant to let me speak to you."

"I can't imagine why."

"She does not seem to understand the principle of doctor-patient confidentiality."

"It's a fairly novel concept here," I sigh, recalling kindly Dr. Macatee, who ratted out a girl in tenth grade dumb enough to ask for birth control.

"I am transferring this call to my receptionist. I want you to make an appointment within the next two weeks."

"I cannot."

He speaks a perfect singsong English that makes you straighten up your own linguistic posture.

"You told me if the samples did not provide a match you wished to explore the possibility of clinical trials, although I must repeat that the safest course is simply to—"

"Actually . . ." I swallow hard. Putting the thought in proper syntax only makes it sound more outlandish. "I have one additional passageway that I have not yet explored."

"Concerning a donor?"

"Yes."

"A family member?"

"Yes."

"Kara, while a bone marrow transplant would be the most desirable form of treatment, it is by no means a necessity. You can simply wait to see how the radiation and chemotherapy—"

"I have to go, Dr. Vallomthail."

"Very well. But do take care of yourself."

"I will. I promise."

There is a beep, and I get Esther, the woman who sits out front. No, I tell her, I cannot make an appointment just yet.

"I'm on vacation," I add, relieved to be able to lie again.

"Lucky you." She has a very nasal voice. "It's eighty-five degrees here!"

"Who was that?" Mother demands, as soon as I get downstairs. "One of your foreign-language friends?"

I am still trying to digest the news, which makes following her misguided leaps a chore.

"He's my doctor."

"That's what he claimed. But he talks like Sinbad the Sailor."

"Dr. Vallomthail is a respected MD."

". . . or a delivery boy from a take-out establishment," she mutters, keeping her back to me.

Mother does not eat in the morning. She stands at the stove, ferociously preparing food for Gerald, both his breakfast and the lunch he takes to work.

"Aren't you going to ask what he had to say?"

"Apparently that's between you and him."

"I'm an adult, Ma. He couldn't talk to you."

"Do you still not eat baloney?"

"No. I mean yes, I still do not eat baloney. I have never eaten baloney."

"That's not true. You used to love it. You just don't remember."

"Nobody *loves* baloney."

"Your brother does."

"Dr. Vallomthail says that the samples you gave—"

"Gerald! Will you wake him, please? I can't keep his eggs warm indefinitely."

Yesterday, I could not even climb the stairs. The uncertainty, the way symptoms come and go, makes living with the disease like negotiating an alien landscape. Craters appear, monsters, but also unexpected and inconceivable beauty. You catch a glimpse of the world Adam-and-Eve fresh, brought on by the fear of it slipping from your grasp forever. I knock on the door to his old room and see sunlight coursing down the hallway carpet, sloshing high against the walls.

"Breakfast."

"I'll be right there."

"Thanks for the homecoming gift." I turn the knob. "When did you get in last night?"

"Shh."

He is trying to crawl out from under a broad but shapely back that has a tiger head tattooed between its shoulder blades.

"Oh, beg pardon. Hey, wait a minute, I thought you and she weren't—"

"Quiet," he hisses. "Close the door, will you?"

It is a very elaborate piece of body art. I have seen it once before, bisected by a bikini strap, but never the whole thing at rest, framed by rats' nests of auburn hair.

"I didn't know you were allowed overnight guests."

21

"We were just talking."

"Well, if that's what you call talking, you might want to wipe your 'mouth,'" I drawl, as he finally manages to work himself free.

Delilah, it would seem, has her period, or was, until last night, a virgin.

"Gerald!" Mother screams.

"I'd appreciate a little privacy here."

"Kind of late for that, isn't it? Why isn't she moving?"

"She's tired. She has a lot on her mind."

A feather would be a lot on her mind, I feel like commenting, but instead say:

"It's a beautiful piece of work."

He is pogoing himself into jeans, but pauses to admire along with me.

"Says she wants it off now."

"No way."

"Tattoo regret."

"Gerald regret."

"She broke up with me."

They always do. He always has this hurt, puzzled look, another opportunity to shrug, while some furious girl hurls various objects—cheap gifts he has bought her, socks he has left in her bed—onto our lawn. But having a tattoo removed is more of a statement, throwing that back in his face.

"What did you do to her?"

"Nothing."

"This nothing have a name?"

"No."

"Why? This nothing fifteen or something?"

"It's not like that. It's not a sexual thing."

With that confusing statement, he herds me out, while Delilah continues to drool on his pillow. Of course he does not have to tell me to stay silent around Mother. Aiding and abetting each other's transgressions is the glue that has kept us together all these years.

"Look at the time," she complains. "I've got to go. There's your breakfast. And I made you each a sandwich."

"Why'd you make me a sandwich?" I protest.

"Gerald, you're taking your sister with you, today. She can't be left alone."

"That's ridiculous."

"You could fall. Or have another spell, like last night."

"What happened last night?" he frowns.

"Nothing."

"She rendered useless the bowl I made in my adult education pottery class."

"I did not render it useless. I was just sick into it."

"You think I could ever serve from that again?"

She is on her way out.

"I am not going to sit in the front room of a tattoo parlor all day."

"Gerald!" she threatens.

"Yes, ma'am," he calls. "I'll look after her."

"The hell you will," I glower.

We listen to her close the front door and lock it behind, as if she could still shut us in, the way she used to when she sold real estate all weekend and we were too small to reach the bolt.

"—not coming to your sorry-ass store," I confirm. "No offense."

He wolfs down eggs and bacon with the same uncritical enthusiasm I imagine he brings to that snoring concubine of his upstairs.

"My doctor called this morning."

"And?"

"The results came back. Those tissue samples you and Ma gave are not a match."

He stares, a forkful of potato suspended halfway. I would reach out, but then remember where that bulging shoulder of his has been.

"It was always a long shot," I sigh.

"Still . . ."

"That leaves Dad's side of the family."

"We back to that again?"

"It's why I'm here."

"If she knew anything, she'd tell you, Kara."

"Can you honestly see spending three years with a person and not having the subject of *who he was* come up from time to time?"

"If Ma could do anything to help, she would."

"She knows something. I'm certain of that."

"That's just your imagination, running wild."

"See, she hoped one of you would be a match. Then she wouldn't have to tell me."

"Tell you what?"

"I don't know! Something about Father. Something we're not supposed to be aware of. It's a game, to her."

"It's not a game. If she—"

"—but she doesn't know who she's playing against." I lean forward. "Now here's the deal: I envision a two-pronged assault. One is interrogating the locals, pumping them for information."

"The locals. You mean me?"

"For my other avenue of inquiry, I need your help."

"I am not getting between you and her."

"All I'm asking is for some mail to be delivered to your store."

"Jerr? Is she gone?" a voice upstairs whines.

"Yes," he answers, still staring. "You always think there's some big mystery, Kara. That there's some secret to unlock. But maybe there's nothing. Did you ever think of that? Nothing more to know."

"There's always more to know."

"You have any sanitary products, hon?"

"Any what?"

"Hall bathroom. Under the sink," I call.

24

Delilah Samson's legs appear, but do not come down. She crouches so her face peeks over the top of the bannister.

"Kara? I didn't know you were back. You didn't tell me Kara was back," she accuses.

Gerald resumes shoveling his eggs.

"How's your mamma?" she asks, very Southern lady, despite being mostly naked. She is holding a piece of cloth to her chest. It is the size of a dishrag. What she was wearing last night, no doubt.

"You just missed her."

"I know. I always just miss her. Jerr won't let the two of us sit down together."

. . . because only one of you would get up, I answer silently.

It is a mystery to me why Mother refuses to acknowledge Gerald's relationship with Delilah. Perhaps she senses how serious it could be.

"Mmm, that smells good."

"Got a sandwich here." I hold up mine. "Baloney."

He glares.

"I'll be right down."

"Under the bathroom sink," I remind her, somewhat pointedly.

There is an argument to be made that the historical past does not exist. If I state, say, that the Battle of Hastings took place in 1066, what I am really claiming is that if I went to a library and looked up the relevant documents, I could determine to a fair amount of certainty that such an event happened on such and such a date. But what I am describing is an action that takes place in the *future*.

Similarly, the silence with which Mother met all my questions—from the time I was old enough to be aware—about our father, what did that imply but a *future* spent trying to learn everything I could about the man? My previous investigations took place mostly in the realm of idle speculation. Now I am motivated by more than curiosity. Vallomthail speaks of my "chances," but I am not interested in chance. I am interested in certainty. I need to be cured. Obviously, a bone marrow transplant from a family member is the only solution. Mother, however, when I first broached the subject, threw up her hands. Father never talked about kin, she insisted. Or his childhood. All he cared about was his family, "meaning you and Gerald." It does not seem natural to me.

"I don't care if he was a rapist or a murderer or even a Mexican," I told her. "I need to find out where he grew up."

"He was none of those things." Her face darkened. "If he had demons in his past, that is where he chose to keep them. He was a good and decent man. I'm so sorry to disappoint you."

But I will find out, one way or the other. This is not the first time we have butted heads. She does not like being dictated to any more than I. Clearly though, my agenda outweighs hers.

I quicken my pace.

The Home is a low, flat, institutional building deliberately placed on the outskirts of town, where the road begins to lose its sense of purpose and the sidewalk is replaced by an intermittently trodden path. There is a circle drive out front, as if horse-drawn carriages once pulled up here for grand affairs, or so I used to pretend when I volunteered every day after school. Once you push open the door, though, there is nothing but miles of cracked linoleum. The residents are left mostly to their own devices, which means they are parked at various angles or doze in the solarium, a windowed room that looks out over a hog farm.

When I find Miss Pitts, she fairly erupts from of her office, pushing piles of paper aside to give me a kiss on the cheek.

"Look at you!" She stands back like I should twirl. "Well, I declare!"

Miss Pitts is a homely woman with goiterous eyes and terrible teeth, but that is not the reason I fight the impulse to shrink when she squeezes my hand. It took years of working at the Senior Center to understand what it was about Justine Pitts that put me off. Then one day it was so apparent that I did not even realize it, not as some lightning bolt of perception. It was more accepting a truth that had been there all along. Miss Pitts had a crush on me. And I, of course, was appalled by anyone who could harbor feelings for such a hideous creature as myself.

"You have not changed one bit," she pronounces, with the fervor of telling an absolute lie.

"Neither have you." I point to the desk and its eternal pile of work. "Business is still good, I see."

"Alas," she answers simply, then brightens. "But there are many residents who remember you, Kara. You made such an impression. I was telling your mother just the other day that I want to have a social, maybe ice cream in the lounge, to celebrate your return."

"I'm just visiting. It isn't really a return."

"They'd be so glad to see you. I—" She puts her fingers to her throat. She is partial to dramatic gestures. "I am so glad to see you."

"Well, I'm glad to see you too, Miss Pitts."

"I believe you can call me Justine, now. After all, you're a grown woman."

"I thought I might just wander around a bit. Stop when I see a familiar face."

"Oh no. You're not escaping my clutches that easily. You're staying right here. We're going to catch up."

With a weary smile I allow her to clear more papers and forcibly sit me down. She produces from a cabinet two room-temperature cans of Coca-Cola Classic.

"My sole vice," she twinkles, handing one over.

. . . the sad thing about that being how it is probably accurate.

"So." She settles back in her chair. "Philosophy."

"Yes."

"What a fascinating subject. The meaning of life. Of existence. What is truth? What is real?"

"This sure hits the spot."

"And what is it about philosophy that interests you?"

"I'm good at it."

"I see."

She waits for more.

"What about you, Miss Pitts? Are you still out on Bangetter Road?"

"Where else would I be?"

"Don't you ever get tired of taking care of these folks?"

"No," she answers with clear-eyed surprise. "Why would I?"

"Because half of them don't even know you're here."

"I don't do it for their appreciation. I do it because it needs being done."

"But at the end of the day . . ."

"There is no end of the day," she sighs, motioning to the stacks of paper. "To be honest, it's gotten a lot worse since you were here. Funding is down. Costs are up. But never for a moment do I doubt the worthiness of what we accomplish."

"That's nice."

"It is, though, a bit lonely-making. So few people understand."

Such a naked appeal for sympathy has the opposite of its intended effect. It steels me, reminds me of my purpose in coming.

"I wonder if I could ask you a personal question. Personal about me, I mean."

"Why, certainly."

"Do you know anything about my father?"

"Who?"

"My daddy. When my mother moved back to Witch's Falls with us, surely there must have been talk."

"Why, no. All I remember is that he was deceased, wasn't he?"

"Yes. An industrial accident."

"What a shame."

"But a young woman goes away, then returns a widow, with two small children, there must have been some gossip about what happened, about her husband, where he—"

"None that I recall."

"Stanley Bell," I try, hoping to strike some kind of spark. "He worked on oil platforms in the Gulf? They never came here the whole time they were courting? You never met him?"

"He'd have been so proud," she sobs, then takes a deep chug of Coke, as if it were vodka. Her face looks even more blotchy and ravaged. "I've missed you, Kara. You say you're just here on a visit? Your mother led me to believe you were staying longer. I was so looking forward to that."

"It's still undetermined," I hear myself answer.

. . . then furiously chastise my brain. It is not "undetermined." Why am I lying? To throw this lonely woman a bone? One that will only cause her redoubled distress when I do, in fact, leave? Or is it myself I am talking to, in the guise of mindless chit-chat? Because if I do not find what I have come for, what exactly is the point of returning up North and listening to Vallomthail assure me my chances are "fair," of resuming my studies at Columbia in the hopes of completing a *five-year* program?

"This isn't really the time or place," she says, "but we should sit down and have a heart-to-heart talk, one day."

"I'd like that."

"From the moment I saw you—" She makes a show of mastering her emotions. Embarrassed, I look away. I cannot help but notice how old everything in this poky little office is. The computer, the telephone. Even the framed photos have undergone that shift where unsuspected bands of color come to the fore, making a mockery of their ostensible subjects. "—I knew you were destined for something special."

A chill contracts my spine. Miss Pitts lives in an atmosphere of perpetual mortality. The seeming ease, almost forwardness, with which she now addresses me, is that because I am a "grown woman" or because, with her long experience in these matters, she can smell it on me, the stink of an early demise? Is that the "something special" I am destined for, the unique quality I possess that gives her, sitting here leering at me, such a ghoulish thrill?

I walk the halls with the same insincere altruistic air I brought to this job as a teen. I did not come five days a week out of selfless love or civic virtue. I came because it was part of my plan. Community service. Sure, every applicant to an Ivy League school helped dig toilets in Guatemala or hammered in nails on a house for some unfortunate, but three solid years helping at the Old Folks Home? That had to stand out. Not to mention a glowing description of my character from Miss Pitts, which I actually had to get her to tone down. Initially, it made me sound like a cross between Mother Theresa and a soft-core porn star.

But whatever my motivation, I did it, and did it well, and got something out of it. Old people have a drastically different take on reality. They live in a foreshortened universe where the past does not exist as a sealed-off entity but caves in on them, burying them beneath tons of debris, or gasses them invisibly, until they choke on sights only they can see. Watching this helped me discard conventional notions about Time, showed me how events never really pass. It also allowed me to *feel* . . . with total strangers, witnesses who could never be called upon to testify in regards to my humanity.

I decide to try my luck with Mr. Robbins. He is in his usual spot, parked at the vending machine so as to get a better view of the trash bins by the side wall. He is an unpleasant man, insofar as you can make judgments about one whose brain is damaged, but I seek him out because of his black tongue. In the past, he would motion me over, get me to sit close, and then tell outrageous lies about his fellow inmates. At first, I dismissed him as a senile creep, but, as I got older and began to understand what adults were capable of, many of the stories he told me became all too plausible. I never liked him, though. He was a butcher, and still looks it, with big meaty hands and a shrewd stare like he is deciding how to best carve you up. He also has a tendency to wet himself, as a triumphant act, only when being cared for by a female attendant.

"Mr. Robbins, it's Kara Bell. Remember me?"

If he sees me at all, he does not let on, though I am standing right in front of him.

"I used to work here as an aide." I hop up on the sill, nestling against its sun-warmed stone, trying to act girlish, also to keep a safe distance from his gray pants. "Jean Bell's daughter. We used to talk."

It is pathetic that, if I really want something, I still rely on flirtation, especially in situations that certainly do not call for it, like with this incontinent old man, or the time I caught myself giggling like a brainless floozy while on the phone to some IT guy in India. In real life, of course, with anyone I am even remotely sensing interest from, my knee-jerk reaction is the opposite, to mimic a frozen popsicle.

"She's a shepherd!" he points.

I look over my shoulder, half expecting to see a flock of merinos led by a woman with a crooked staff. Instead there are the same battered old cans (still metal, that is how old and unchanged this place remains) with their lids either toppled off or sitting rakishly askew, baking in the sun.

"I've come to visit. I have some questions for you."

31

He shifts in his chair, trying to look past me.

"Mr. Robbins?"

"You got nothing!" he bellows.

Anywhere else, that would cause people to turn, but shouts and screams are the daily atmosphere of the place, the clank of human machinery slowly falling apart. He reaches up to his head and giggles, very mincingly, like he is a woman, pretending to plump out an invisible curl.

"Oh, my hair, you mean? That's right. I got nothing. It's gone. I lost it."

"Lost it!" he laughs.

It does seem comic, for an instant, as if I could simply misplace my life. That, however, is not as easy as it sounds. Cancer, I have discovered, only accentuates your dilemma, rather than replacing it with a new one.

"I lost my head. Or found it, rather."

I tilt so he can feast his fill on my bare skull.

But his expression falls flat. His mind shuts down. That happens. The power cuts out with no warning.

"I came because I want to ask you about my mother, Jean Bell. And her husband, Stanley."

He is a blank. His face could be a cliff, solid rock, holes slashed for each eye, through which bulge a kind of thinking slime.

"You've been in town longer than anyone." I lean forward, crossing my legs. "And you know everything, you used to tell me."

"Tell you," he says softly.

"Yes. All about people. About their lives."

"Tell you," he says again.

"Do you remember when Jean Bell came back here after her marriage? With two small children? A boy and a girl?"

"Bell," he confirms.

"That's right. But it's Stanley Bell I'm wondering about. Her husband. Did you ever meet him? Or did you ever hear tell of him? Where he came from? If he had any relations someone here might have known?"

"You mean Jeannie! Jeannie Simmons!"

"That's right! Simmons was her maiden name."

In fact, Mother is driven apoplectic when people called her Jeannie. "It is *Jean*," she sounds out carefully, as if English is their second, or maybe fifth, language.

"She was a real hunk of woman, Jeannie Simmons."

"Don't I know it?" I pretend to be one of his lecherous cronies. I would even go so far as to nudge him in the ribs were I not afraid of crushing several. "But Stanley Bell, her husband, did anyone know him? Or know of him? Did she ever mention—?"

"She was built like a brick shithouse."

"Uh-huh." I try to unclench my jaw. "But the man she was married to, her late husband, did you ever hear anyone—?"

"Pretty walking away as coming through the door, know what I mean?"

"Do tell."

"Who'd you say you were again?"

"I'm her daughter."

"Whose?"

"Johnny! Look at you!"

One of the aides has happened by and noticed his trousers have that distinctive shadow to them.

"Not again, Johnny! Are we going to have to start putting you in diapers?" she threatens. "You don't want that, do you?"

"Depends who puts 'em on," he cackles, looking at me with those gross butcher's eyes. "Jeannie Simmons. So you're back."

"No, I ain't her," I say, giving up.

"Sure you are. Back in town. I knew who you were the minute you walked in."

"I got to get him changed."

"Depends who puts 'em on!" he wheezes, as she wheels him off. Then he looks over his shoulder and calls, "Can't keep away, can you?"

CHAPTER THREE

The creek is nothing but a drainage ditch. It comes out of the state park, but by the time it wends its way through the bad side of Witch's Falls it has been polluted by the processing plants and served as a receptacle for any trash the carting companies won't take away. I remember finding, on one of my rambles, an old oxygen tank wedged tight in the exposed roots of a tree. Christy and I once came upon a bed, rusted, without a mattress, but still boasting a carved headboard, sitting squarely in the middle of the current.

Walking along its "banks" is too grand a description of what I do, which is basically hop in and out of its way, finding stones or holding onto overhanging branches when the sides are steep. It becomes, for a time, a culvert, where you cannot see anything but earthen walls and foamy, suspiciously green waters. Then the land flattens out and the surface more resembles a pool, dotted with appliances and tires. Some of the houses here are elaborate in an added-on way. "Not up to code," I remember Mother sniffing, and that is certainly true. They are what lies behind the code, evidence of naked thought, as if you daydreamed a house and there it was, with no intervening blueprints or reference to the laws of gravity.

Mae and Horace's place is a prime example. There must be some kernel it is built around, a shack or prim little cottage, but buried so deep in accumulated rooms, hallways, sheds, and outlying porches that you would be hard-pressed to pick it out. I, for one, have never penetrated the interior. The porch, on the creek side, is three-quarters enclosed and practically a separate entity unto itself, a kind of general store with refrigerator, reach-in freezer, and a bright yellow sign that reads BAIT.

"Anything I should look out for?" I call.

They plant in front of their house. Mostly vegetables, but medicinal herbs too, which are harder to see. Those are what I am afraid of stepping on.

"Anything hasn't come up by now, you're not going to kill," Horace answers.

Nevertheless, I step carefully. There are patches, rather than rows, of various crops, most of which I recognize. One circle is noticeable for an absence of greenery. It is just overturned dirt.

"Red," he says, following my gaze.

"No."

"Got hit. Last week."

"That's terrible."

"Dumbest dog," he says tenderly. "I'm still figuring out what to put on top of him."

"You mean a stone?"

"—thought maybe yams."

The stairs are coming away from the porch. I leap onto the pine planks as if boarding a ship.

"I didn't recognize you," Mae says.

I give her a hug, grateful for the honesty. If only the world would stop lying to me. Of course then I would have to return the favor, which is a fairly terrifying proposition.

"Who else would it be?" I joke.

36

She is a big woman, but fast and strong. I have seen her chase after hedgehogs, brandishing a club like you would see a caveman do in a comic strip. I have also seen her stare down an Arkansas state trooper cruiser, its lights flashing, its siren doing that low growl, when they came looking for A.C. But if she can, she sits, in a tube-and-vinyl office chair that tumbled downstream one spring, during the floods.

Horace, too, is no slouch when it comes to activity. He has a green thumb. He also hunts small game from the surrounding forest, which almost no one else around here can do, anymore. He has the frame of a farmer, wiry, with a gaunt face and legs that fold up. I like to think of Mae, Horace, and A.C. as my alternative or anti-family, though they would be shocked to hear me say any such thing.

"Where are your shoes?" Mae asks.

"I left them."

"Up North?"

"At home." Since getting back, my feet have begun to acquire a nice slippery layer of dirt. My toes are learning how to grip again, a childhood feeling. "That's awful, about Red."

"Can't get too attached to a dog." Horace speaks across me, to Mae.

"He just never gave me cause to complain, that's all I said," she answers in a similar tone. They often have a private conversation going, even when you are right in front of them. Now she turns. "You look like you've been doing battle with the Devil."

"Treatments," I correct, though her description, as usual, sounds more apt. "They don't know how successful yet."

"But you're done?"

"For now."

"Praise the Lord." She manages to rock, though the chair is not a rocker. "When I heard you were poorly, I thought, Well, the only good thing about that is it will bring her home."

It is odd how she can express identical sentiments to those of my mother but without making me mad.

"What was it, exactly?" Horace asks.

"Nothing." I know that the word itself, even couched in medical terminology, would not be welcome in their world. "I'm fine, now. How about yourself? How are you-all doing?"

"We're blessed," she pronounces, "although some of us find that hard to accept."

"—thinking about taking a job," Horace translates.

"Doing what?"

"Trucking. Long hauls. A friend of mine bought a rig."

"But who'll take care of the garden?"

"That's just what I say," Mae nods.

"You do a pretty good job."

"I don't do nothing. I just scare things off."

"That's ninety percent of it. We could use the cash," he explains.

"Kara, you want some Grapette?"

"Thank you, no."

The floor is coming up. Angling crazily. Another "spell." I can recognize them fast enough now, maybe because the attacks are not as severe, and translate the motion into something more natural. Just me, lying down. All of a sudden. Fooling no one, but not making a scene, I will my body to stop shaking and stretch out in the sun. My eyes close. I feel her watching me.

"You all right, child?"

"Mmmhmm."

There is a sharp foretaste of death in my throat. I swallow several times, trying to rinse away the fear. Slowly, the urge to be sick recedes.

"You make friends up North?"

"One or two."

"They don't wear shoes either?"

"Everyone wears shoes in Brooklyn."

"—thought maybe you were walking around here this way because all the snakes had left Arkansas and moved on up to New York City."

"No," I smile. "I'm the only snake that's made it that far."

None of this makes a whole lot of sense. Am I even having this conversation? I ask. Yet it is deeply comforting.

"Well, I'm glad to see you," she concludes, "feet and all."

Slowly, the shakes and dizziness pass. The sound of the creek takes them away. A screen door whines. I look up.

A.C. makes a gagging sound as he emerges from the house.

"How come you don't cover those things up, girl?"

"Because then you'd make fun of my shoes."

"Damn straight I would. Least I wouldn't smell 'em, though."

He struts with an air of exaggerated importance, a six-foot-tall would-be rooster, not seeming to realize he is every inch the domesticated fowl.

"Anyone see my ASU shirt? I can't find it anywhere."

"Don't you remember?" Horace says. "We wrapped him up in it."

"Wrapped up who in it?"

"Red."

"You did what?"

A.C. has his father's build, but not Horace's sly humor. And he certainly does not have Mae's rock-solid authority. Instead, he has carved out for himself the role of drama queen.

"There was blood all over. We just grabbed whatever was on the line."

"But that was my ASU shirt."

"—least the people had the decency to bring him home," Mae sighs. "They claim he ran right in front of them."

"Dumbest dog," Horace repeats.

"Well, where is it now? Where's my shirt?"

I should add that he is naked from the waist up and naked from the waist down a great deal too, aping that tired fashion of belting his jeans below the buttocks.

"Where is it?" Horace echoes, fixing his eyes on the grave. "About two feet above the water table, I'd say. Give or take."

"But that's my Wolves shirt. I paid good money for that."

"I'm thinking yams."

"What's the point," Mae snorts, "if you ain't going to be here to tend them?"

"All they require is some light hoeing."

"—dog never gave me cause to complain," she repeats, staring along with him at the spot. "Unlike some."

"I can't believe they buried that filthy mutt in a crucial element of my wardrobe," A.C. complains.

It is dark, and he is driving me home.

"This stuff any good?"

"It's Gold."

"Smells homegrown."

"You smell homegrown. What is with this Nature Girl look of yours?"

"It's not a look."

"Everything's a look."

"It's what I wear."

"You're a disgrace."

"Excuse me for not having a *wardrobe.*"

He has settled, after much consideration, on a skintight *Everything's Better At Walmart* number, immaculately cleaned and pressed. His ostentatiously flaunted boxers are green polka dot.

"A.C., I'm going to need something to get me through these next few weeks, and this stuff smells like hay."

"I also can't believe you didn't bring me a present."

"That was an oversight. I apologize."

"I mean, even a Statue of Liberty would have been nice."

"I was a little busy, dealing with things."

"How's that going? How you feeling?"

"Tip-top."

I do, actually. This last weakness was the briefest and the least nauseating. Being among friends is restorative. I smile over at him. Despite his mincing manner, A.C.'s hands are the most sensual I have ever seen, the way they rest lazily on the steering wheel.

"So what's all this about Horace going away?"

"It's of no interest to me what he does."

"If he goes on the road, then you'll be the man of the house."

He giggles.

I stick my nose into the bag again.

"It's the best I could do on short notice. There's not much call for weed, anymore. Whole business has changed."

"How so?"

"For the worse."

In high school, A.C.'s beanpole physique and bespectacled face gave him the misleading appearance of a brainiac nerd. Nothing could have been further from the truth. It made his infatuations with football players and habitués of the weight room about as comic as my own absurdly repressed pinings. We would commiserate. *Laugh so hard you cry.* That was our motto.

"Cheer up. At least you don't got cancer."

For a moment, I think he is going to stop and throw me out.

"Don't say it! Why'd you have to say it for?"

"Because it's the truth."

"It's wrong, saying it out loud that way. It's bad luck."

"I already got bad luck. How much worse could it be?"

We are taking the long way, just driving, as we so often used to. I am supposed to be sampling the purchase, sharing with him, but he has already indicated he does not want any, which is odd. I fight back a tear. I had not expected such a lack of sympathy.

"You can't get it off a car seat," I grumble.

"That's not what I meant."

"Well, what did you mean?"

"I just don't like you reducing it to the level of one of your jokes, that's all."

"But it is. It's an extra-funny joke."

I can see he does not get it though. Few do. I change the subject.

"Is Horace really going?"

"Looks like it," he sighs. "If the old man hits the road, that means it'll just be Mae and me."

"He'll be back, won't he?"

"Question is, Will I still be here?"

"Why wouldn't you?"

"Like I said, business is bad. Everything's getting disputed. Territory. Customers. There's new people. New suppliers. They're not very civilized."

"Can't you reach some sort of accommodation?"

"You mean like they did with the dog?"

"Red? Horace said he got hit."

"By a thirty-eight. Then they ran him over a few times, for appearance's sake. I guess they didn't want to get Mamma all riled up. That's their idea of accommodation."

"Why would they hurt Red?"

"Just a misunderstanding. It's cleared up. For now."

"You sure you don't want any of this? I imagine you need it."

"I have to keep my wits about me," he mutters, looking both ways, though we are not even at an intersection. "I hear you've been asking about your daddy."

"How'd you hear that?"

He accelerates. I am pinned against the seat.

"Don't you remember how talking to people around here is like putting an ad in the newspaper? If we still had one."

"You know anything?"

"About your daddy? Oh yeah." His hands rest lightly on the wheel. "I know he wouldn't want his daughter looking like she dresses from the Goodwill, passing her time with the nigs who run the Bait Shop, when she should be far away from here, getting herself an education."

"—terrified of dying," I whisper, just to hear how the words sound out loud.

"What?"

"Nothing."

His strangely ineffective headlights illuminate wall after wall of white fog.

Before leaving New York, I sold all my electronic devices. Mother misunderstood. She thought it was some grand farewell . . . to Life, I suppose. In fact, it was the opposite. I saw, in vision cleansed by the poison burning its way through my veins, that these so-called miracles of technology did nothing but *impede* thought. They chivvied it down predictable paths, completed a sentence not with an eye toward the truth but swerved the underlying impulse back to the stalest convention. "Friends" made, "texts" produced, "searches" undertaken, were parodies of what those words originally meant, brutal reminders to stay within the herd, the lowing mass, all of us lumbering obediently toward intellectual extinction. Cancer, horrible as it is, scraped away the film coating my eyes. It laid my heart bare, so now that organ's beat sometimes deafens me.

But this newfound acuity I feel is on the inside. It seems to make no difference in the Kara others perceive, and so widens the gap between the two. The result is that my time back here has left me even less certain of who I am. Everyone I meet addresses a self I

43

barely recognize. "She" seems to be polite, gracious, and ready to settle down, fit into the community, perhaps as a librarian or low-level clerk at the Town Hall, the kind who helps you fill out forms. My pretensions to learning, to graduating summa cum laude, to having been the youngest person ever awarded the prestigious Loeb Fellowship in Philosophical Studies, are seen as a particularly silly form of showing off. No one mentions my condition except in disparaging, dismissive terms, as if contracting lymphoma was an unfortunate accident, and my five-o'clock-shadow scalp a Yankee-inspired fashion faux pas.

"Is that what you'd call punk?" Delilah asks.

"I guess. Or neo-Nazi, maybe."

I am puzzled to find her in front, sitting on the permanently extended Barcalounger. She is a good advertisement for the place though, with her Eye of the Tiger tattoo nosing through the back of a slutty halter top.

"What's he doing there?"

"A cross." She shows her disapproval. She has a not unattractive pouty face and a body already expressing its desire for motherhood. "I tried to interest the gentleman in one of those Rosicrucian designs, but he was afraid his pastor might object."

I cluck sympathetically.

"Gerald can do crosses in his sleep. He's not challenged enough. That's my main concern."

"And what about you, Delilah? Are you still working at Kreski's?"

"No. I waitress at The Best, five nights a week."

"What's The Best?"

"Haven't you heard? It's this new restaurant out on the highway. The Best Steakhouse in Witch's Falls."

"What's it called?"

"I just told you. The Best Steakhouse in Witch's Falls. They're all over. There's one in Ouajita, one in Hot Springs."

I have read and understood Edmund Husserl in his superficially clear yet astoundingly difficult German, but this is beyond me.

"How can you have a restaurant called The Best Steakhouse in Witch's Falls when it's in Ouajita?"

"It's The Best wherever it is," she explains patiently. "The Best Steakhouse in Booneville. The Best Steakhouse in Hot Springs. But each is the same. The same layout, menu, everything. They're a chain, I guess. Or a franchise?"

The storefront is a collection of discarded furniture. There is the busted Barcalounger, a few unmatched chairs, and a cigarette-scarred table on which thick binders of various designs are scattered. Gerald's more recent creations are tacked to the walls. I notice he has started doing nature scenes: the sun going down over mountains, a river with trees on either side, although there is still plenty of the usual stuff as well, religious iconography, maudlin memorials, wishful sex dreams. The bread and butter of the business.

"He should get out," she declares. "That's what I keep telling him."

"Get out of body art?"

"No. Out of town. He should go west, to San Diego or Los Angeles. He could get hired in one of the shops, there. He's really good."

"But where would that leave you?"

"I mean him and me, both."

I try not to look surprised by her proprietary tone. According to Gerald, they are broken-up, although still sleeping together. But that is not how she talks.

"Leaving home's not for everyone."

"It worked for you, didn't it?"

"I suppose. What does Gerald think about all this?"

"Oh, you know Jerr. He's a good boy. He wouldn't want to abandon your mamma."

"Of course not."

"But now that you're back . . ."

I have been flipping through the designs. There is one that reads, in bold blocky letters: YOUR FAVORITE BAND SUCKS.

"I didn't know you two were that serious."

"Serious as cancer," she retorts, then realizes what she has said and claps a hand over the gaping O of her mouth.

"That's OK."

"I am so sorry, Kara. I don't know what I was thinking."

"No offense taken."

She, however, seizes the opportunity to turn this into some kind of ice-breaker moment.

"It just feels so right," she confesses. "Jerr and me."

"That's nice. I thought maybe there was some kind of problem?"

"That's in the past, now. We hit a rough spot, but I just decided to put it out of my head. I let go of my anger."

"Good for you."

"Does he ever say anything about us?"

"We don't talk about those things."

"I just know it's going to work out. Life has a way of arranging itself. There's some Force, operating. That's what I believe. Like with my name."

"What about your name?"

"It's Delilah," she says, as if we have just met. "Delilah Samson. As in Samson and Delilah."

"Yes?"

"Well, what are the odds on that just happening all by itself? On it occurring by chance, I mean? That's why I believe there's some kind of overarching Spirit influencing our ways. Bringing things together. Bringing people together too."

"But your name . . ." I am once again confused. "Your parents picked your name."

"Yes. But they didn't know."

"Sure they did. They knew that if their last name was Samson, and they called you Delilah—"

"Nuh-uh," she stubbornly insists. "My daddy said it never occurred to either one of them. It just happened. Delilah. Delilah Samson."

"Well, I'll be."

"But if we get married . . ." She shrugs her bare shoulders. "I don't know what I'll do."

"Name-wise?"

"Yes."

You could change your first name to Dumb, I almost suggest. Then you would be Mrs. Dumb Bell.

This whole time, we have been hearing the buzz of the electric needle. Now Gerald comes out. Delilah, I notice, deals with the money and paperwork and post-care instructions, like she is co-owner.

"Where's that?" I ask, pointing to one of his new designs. It is a seascape, a big wave, curling, so well done it seems almost three-dimensional, and in permanent motion.

"No place in particular."

"You don't work from pictures?"

"In my head." He taps his temple, like there is an actual section, an area of the brain. "Here you go."

He opens a drawer and hands me an envelope.

"Thanks."

"I still don't understand why you need to have stuff sent here."

"I told you. It's personal."

"She won't go sneaking through your room."

"That isn't my room. It's a diorama."

"We've been having such a good talk," Delilah calls.

Even though I am on Gerald's side—unquestioningly and always—it bothers me, what he is doing. If he is seeing some other

47

woman, he should not be stringing this one along. I do not want to see my baby brother become another small-town philanderer.

"Delilah told me about The Best."

"The Best Steakhouse? What about it?"

"How it's all over. How there's more than one."

"I wouldn't know."

"Of course you do, honey," she says, hooking her arm through his. "There's one in Ouajita, one in Booneville . . ."

"So you could go from one to the other, have yourself a good time, and always be eating at The Best, but a different one every night."

"Now why would he want to do that?" she giggles. "Might as well go to the closest."

"She's got a point," I nod, trying to widen my eyes significantly.

"I don't know what you're talking about."

"Wouldn't want to get caught patronizing the wrong establishment, just for a change. Especially when it's pretty much the same food, no matter where you end up."

"Besides, I slip him extra fries."

"That would be kind of like cheating on the homegrown product, wouldn't it?"

"Just what is it you're up to?" He nods to the mail. "Who do you know at the Texas Department of Vital Records?"

"I told you, it's part of my master plan."

"Don't tell her I had any part in it."

"I won't." I smile toward Delilah. "All your secrets are safe with me."

"What secrets? What's she talking about, Jerr?"

"She has her own way of expressing herself," I hear him say, as he closes the door behind me.

Where to go? The sun is beating down. It is ninety-eight in the shade, and there is no shade except for what is provided by the gazebo, a tilting wooden structure plopped dead center in the park opposite the War Memorial. Excited, I pad my way over burning pavement and uncut grass, reveling in the textures, reveling in the pain that travels up through my newly formed layers of calloused sole.

To be alive!

I almost shout it out.

You could always fit back in as Town Eccentric, part of me proposes.

No, I answer. That would be too much like picking up where I left off.

It is less cluttered than I remember. In high school, the popular kids used to come here after dark. Beer cans, cigarette butts, and, very daringly, the occasional condom wrapper, were evidence of their wild times. There must be similar evidence now, but I no longer see it. My eyes are trained to pick out different clues, such as the way the sides of the octagon do not line up, do not meet properly, revealing seams of emptiness significant as the walls themselves.

The death certificate was not hard to track down. Texas allows copies to adult-age offspring. And here it is, what they have all been trying to keep from me—

Stanley K. Bell

—but typed under "Birthplace of Decedent" is

Unknown.

My hopes are once again dashed. I had fantasized it would be a hamlet, up in the hills, so I could make some calls and find a Chatty Cathy at the local Agway who would like nothing better than to gossip all about the Bells, remember my daddy, "such a bright boy," and shake her head in sympathy when I explain what happened to him. Then she gives me the names and numbers of his brothers and sisters, and their children too, my cousins, a veritable cornucopia of DNA. Instead, it is just another dead end.

My eyes, which have been trying to avoid it, cannot help now but go back up to the top and linger over "crushed chest and thorax, massive internal injuries." My father was killed when a giant metal hook swung loose and smashed into his side. Mother had been living with us in rented rooms along the coast while he was away for weeks at a time on different jobs. With the death settlement money, she moved back to the house she had grown up in. Her parents were recently deceased. Her children were three and one, respectively. The photocopied paper is so flimsy. I finger it, try to extract information through physical touch. I feel something more is here, but I am not seeing it. I need to get my brain back in motion. But *thought*, in the sense I employ the word, as a tool of critical investigation, is exactly what I am feeling less and less capable of doing. Is it the heat? The illness? The company? Maybe there is a different kind of intelligence, I consider, more a creeping form of emotional inquiry, that is just as valid as sifting through facts and following logical chains of argument, as long as the end result is the same: knowledge. But how do you grab ahold of something so amorphous as feeling? Where do you start?

CHAPTER FOUR

"Why do we have to drive?"

"It's more seemly."

"Seemly? You want to be noticed coming to church in an Oldsmobile Cutlass Supreme? That confers some kind of status?"

I am back in the nest again, watching an empty bottle of Snapple Kiwi Cooler roll from one side of the seat well to the other. My body, clad just about as uncomfortably as is humanly possible, sweats through pantyhose, borrowed heels, and one of the fifty new bras.

"How does it fit?" she asks, watching me tug.

"Like a fucking harness."

"Kara! Will you watch your mouth? We're almost there."

My revenge is that I refuse to wear a bonnet or whatever ridiculous headgear she had hoped to cram my unsightly scalp into. Still, I wonder why I so weakly acquiesced to coming, especially when Gerald could still be heard snoring away. I suppose his soul is not in such immediate peril.

"In answer to your question, I was afraid you might become exhausted."

"It's only a half mile."

"You couldn't even climb the stairs when you first got here."

"That was before your nursing restored me to health."

"You do seem to have gained a little weight." She risks a look over. "I think being home agrees with you. Or maybe . . ."

"Maybe what?"

"Maybe that doctor of yours made a mistake. Maybe this disease is not as serious as you think. I mean, exactly where did he go to medical school? He barely speaks a word of English."

"He speaks English the way it was intended to be spoken."

"Maybe on the moon."

What would Jesus do? I silently rehearse.

It is a calming technique.

Growing up, I was encouraged to pose that question when faced with a moral or ethical dilemma. Forced reading of the gospels gave me a fair idea of His personality. I took the advice literally.

What would Jesus do if His mother had refused Him potentially valuable information concerning His genetic inheritance?

It is not as outrageous a scenario as one might first suppose. Was not His search for the truth, regarding parentage, just as crucial as mine? Did He not, in effect, need a cosmic bone marrow transplant in order to triumph over the forces of Death? Will my Father, too, forsake me?

Viewed psychologically, what Jesus did, of course, was take out His frustrations on everyone else. He scourged the temple, cursed the fig tree, and generally made Himself a royal pain in the ass, because no one would tell Him what He wanted to know.

A course of action eerily similar to my own, I conclude. It is good to confirm I am on the right track.

"I got Dad's death certificate."

"You did what?"

"It didn't say where his birthplace was."

"Why would you want to know that?"

"You know why. So I could track down relatives."

"Are you still riding that hobbyhorse?"

"Mother, this information could save my life."

"I think you're being a tad melodramatic, Kara."

"I don't get it. Are you saying that I'm not even sick?"

"What I am saying is that you have been under a great deal of stress for a very long time. And that place you were living in was so *dirty*, so *busy*, that it may very well have contributed to your condition."

"New York didn't give me cancer."

"That remains to be seen. The important thing is that you've had treatment and you're on the mend. Can't you see it? You definitely have more color in your cheeks. And I also think it helps that you are no longer delving into subjects that, if you'll pardon me for saying so, are probably best left undisturbed."

"What are you taking about?"

"All this *Ding-an-sich* stuff. Once you start reading about it, it seems like a combination of gibberish and black magic. Honestly, I can't believe they offer academic degrees in such things."

"*Ding-an-sich?*" I try to contain my utter amazement. "What the hell do you know about epistemological rationalism?"

"I special-ordered a book you mentioned. *Critique of Pure Reason?*"

"Why did you do that?"

"I try to take an interest in my children's . . . hobbies," she falters, knowing that is the wrong word. "I thought maybe it would help us have more intelligent conversations."

"Aren't you curious about Dad's past? What I might find out?"

"It's the same as me letting Gerald put that little gardenia on my ankle. Even though, really, I feel that the body is a temple and should remain unmarked. But as a parent, I also feel it's important to—"

"Maybe we could go there together."

"Go where?"

"Where he was born. Snoop around. You could talk to people who knew him, find out more about him. It could be fun."

"I don't *know* where he grew up, honey. I told you already. He didn't favor me with that type of information."

"And you never asked?"

"It was not that kind of relationship."

"What do you mean?"

"It was not excessively verbal."

"Well, what did you two do, just grunt like a pair of cavemen?"

She sticks out her hand, still driving, and feels my forehead.

"You may have a fever. I want you to see Dr. Macatee."

"Macatee! Is he still alive?"

"Of course he's still alive. He's our family doctor. Don't you remember?"

"That old quack? Why should I see him?"

"Because he is a brilliant diagnostician."

"I don't need to be diagnosed. I already know what I got."

"Maybe you can talk to him in a way you can't talk to me."

"About what?"

"Kara, I understand why you are so set on this. As a child, you were always questioning, always itching to do something about a problem, never content to sit back. Which I admired. And, of course, when one has a brush with illness—"

"A brush?"

It is all I can do not to grab the wheel and send us crashing into a tree.

"—that tendency to question becomes even more pronounced. I just wonder if this obsession with tracing your father's ancestry isn't a little misguided."

"First you're an amateur philosopher, and now you're a doctor?"

"All I'm saying is maybe this is much ado about nothing."

"You know, don't you? You know where he came from. You just won't tell me. Why?"

"No, I do not know," she says carefully. "And all the wishing in the world is not going to change that. He was a good and decent man. Isn't that enough for you?"

"I need bone marrow, not to be told my daddy shat chocolate ice cream."

"Maybe Macatee can prescribe some medication." We pull into the church parking lot. "Something to elevate your mood."

"The *Ding-an-sich*," I mutter.

The thing-in-itself. Not what we perceive through our senses but what *is*. What we can never know.

I wish I could say that I responded to the Catholic Church's rich intellectual heritage, that I was "raised by Jesuits," as one so often reads of great thinkers, but Saint Archibald's was never much more than a fantastic hide-and-seek venue for me. Its pews, chancel, and vestry provided innumerable nooks to become invisible in, not that anyone else was ever searching for me. Now, of course, hobbled by ridiculous shoes, my legs damp in sausage casing, I am just one more piece of furniture. A little boy squirts past, no more acknowledging my existence than he would that of a coatrack.

Mother reintroduces me all round. I make nice. I have no desire to shame her. There is not a regular priest anymore. Attendance has shrunk so low they only get a circuit-rider who blows into town and hands out the crackers.

"How long are you going to be with us, Kara?" Ilene Casimir asks.

"That depends on my prognosis. They tell me my chances are good, but I've discovered that the science of epidemiology is largely a fraud. For example, when they say the survival rate is eighty percent *after two years*, what they really mean is that when you look at the same bunch of people *after three* years they're all pushing up daisies, or connected to some godforsaken hunk of machinery that—"

"I believe Ilene wants to know how long you plan to be in Witch's Falls," Mother interrupts.

"Oh. Through the summer, at least."

"So you'll be here for the pageant," Martin says.

"What's that?"

"It's a military-style reenactment I'm planning for the town. To encourage civic pride."

"When does it take place?"

"In mid-August. We're still trying to get people. Maybe you'd like to participate."

"I'm not sure Kara is up for that kind of strenuous activity."

"Would I get to fire a gun?"

"A rifle," he corrects. "Absolutely. She could be in Butler's brigade. They were cut up pretty early on. Not much running involved."

"You mean I'd get to play a corpse? That might be good practice."

I myself think this is pretty funny, but nobody else laughs.

"I don't see Christine," Mother observes sweetly.

"She's home with the child."

"They're so fussy at this age."

"We could really use you," Martin says.

"I'll think about it. It was nice to see you the other night."

I like Martin. Everyone likes Martin. The problem is that is pretty much all you can say about him. And you have to keep saying it, to remind yourself, because the impression he makes is so fleeting, like breath on a windowpane. He is tall, blandly good-looking, not lacking in confidence. What is it, then? Money, maybe, having so much, from such a young age, that it kind of took the edge off him. Being raised by a matron like Ilene could not have

56

helped, either. She reminds me of a real comfy sofa. By comparison, his father, who developed a lot of properties around here, was a tiny man. I suppose he was one of those tufted throw pillows that you set on top of the sofa. Purely ornamental. Yet he was the one who made the fortune and was, by all accounts, a shark of a businessman. Go figure.

"Christy misses you," he says.

"Looks like she has her hands full with Shelby."

"Shelby-From-Hell-Be. That's what she calls him."

"Martin," Ilene chastises. "You should come to the house more often, Kara. Especially during the day. I think you could be a steadying influence."

"I hear Shelby likes lima beans," I answer, somewhat at a loss. No one has ever called me a steadying influence before.

"It's hard for a new mother. You remember, Jean."

"Oh yes."

"Particularly for an only child like Christine. I don't think she's entirely comfortable with the domestic life. It doesn't suit her temperament."

"Maybe Kara could teach her to be more philosophical," Martin jokes.

As we settle down, Mother reaches into her pocketbook and produces a black circle of cloth.

"What's that?"

"Just put it on."

"Ma, do you know what this is?"

"It's a skullcap. I feel you should have some covering on your head in the House of God."

"Other people don't."

"Other people have *hair*, honey. I hate to be so blunt, but it's disrespectful not to—"

"This is a yarmulke, Ma."

"I know what it is. The pope wears one. I've seen it. And if it's good enough for the Holy Father, I don't see why you can't make one tiny concession to decency and wear it during the service."

"Where did you get a yarmulke?"

"That is not the point!"

"OK, OK." I put the thing on. It is like a third bra cup. "Are you dating a Jew?"

"If I had to listen to one more minute of that evil woman trying to use you to further her own nefarious schemes . . ."

"What are you talking about?"

". . . telling you to drop on by Martin's house. 'Especially in the daytime.' Ilene has never liked Christy, that's for sure. And now that she's got a grandson out of the deal, she's looking for ways to make mischief between those two so she can have the little Heir Apparent all to herself."

"You cannot be serious."

"Why not? We both know what Christy Lee's like. She's the Pied Piper of Fornication."

A surge of electricity goes through me.

"You sure know how to excite a girl," I say.

"There's bad blood over there, I'm telling you." She reaches over and tries to make me look a little less like a rabbi. "I just don't want you getting hurt."

At this point, the couple behind us creaks their pew slightly, which is a genteel way of calling for quiet.

"I don't take communion, anymore," I warn.

"I'm not surprised," she breathes back. "With what you've been up to, the wafer would probably turn to hot lead in your mouth."

After, as always, we go to the cemetery. She keeps the plot immaculate, passing her hand over the stone in loving fashion.

"I used to come here and talk," she says. "Tell him what was going on. Then, one day, I didn't sense his presence anymore. Not in a listening way."

"Maybe he got bored."

"It's possible. Our earthly concerns must seem petty to those in heaven." She sits on the grass and takes a deep breath. "Since you're so determined, I'll tell you what little I know. Even though it seems like violating a confidence. Your father regarded the past as a closed book. He was a drinker, or had been. He'd quit by the time I met him. He'd done some bad things, I suppose. Things he was ashamed of. He didn't want to talk about them, and I didn't want to hear. I had my own past, which also didn't bear close examination. You might say we had a mutual agreement not to question each other too closely. We decided our lives would begin with one another."

"And all the time you were together he never mentioned growing up, being a child, having brothers and sisters?"

"I already told you. It was not that kind of relationship." She lies back and stares up at the sky. "If you must know, it was intensely sexual."

I am not even sure I hear her right.

"Your father was a very virile man. Very manly."

"That's nice."

"He was a stallion," she enunciates, seeming to ogle some unsavory cloud formation directly overhead.

"Mother, I have absolutely no interest in hearing—"

"It was not a question of his endowment, which was . . . fine, but of his *energy*. Of his *persistence*."

"If you keep talking this way, I'm going to have to wait in the car."

"My name for him was Septimus."

I look at the tombstone to make sure we are talking about the same person.

"It's the Latin word for *seven*."

"*Seventh*," I correct automatically.

"Close enough."

"When did you take Latin?"

"In high school. I was quite good at it."

"But why call him Septimus? Was he the seventh child in his family?"

"It was my bedroom name for him."

"Oh." I still don't understand. Then I do. "Oh."

She gets to her feet and brushes herself off.

"See, you say you want information, but when you get it, when I share something dear with you, something that I have never told another soul in my entire life, you don't know what to do with it. You don't know where to file it away in that super-organized brain of yours. That's something you might want to work on, while you're down here."

She walks off, leaving me to contemplate a rather icky picture, or several pictures—seven, to be precise—presented in rapid succession, like time-lapse photography.

"Eew," I tell the stone.

The Raggedy Ann doll has a heart drawn on her chest. You can see it if you pull down the dress's neckline. It is printed onto the flesh-colored fabric and reads, *I Love You*. Mother told me Father once drew the same heart on his chest and showed it to me, I was so attached to that doll. "In red Magic Marker. It took forever to come off." Of course I remember nothing.

I linger in bed, listen to the sound of water in the pipes, squirrels' paws on the roof, a pan clanging against the stovetop. Are they in there, malignant cells, replicating? Is that awful buzz what passes for the ambient noise of morning inside my body? I cannot live with such vulnerability. As a child, I used to be fascinated by my otherness. It seemed amazing that I was an individual. Logically, it made no sense. I was formed of the same stuff, subject to the same laws, yet felt so intensely apart. It was, in fact, my only feeling, the only concept my brain recognized as worthy of the name. I was a soap bubble whose fragile surface—the very property that made it what it was—refused to pop. I could never say if I wanted it to or not. Rejoining the surrounding universe had an undeniable appeal. It would be like coming home. Acceptance. But the shifting prismatic patterns that colored my perception of the world, my deliciously flexible magical border, how could I do anything but embrace that which made me unique? And now I face its very real extinction.

Mother leaves first, her heels punishing the cement walkway, her car door slamming shut. She warms up the engine forever. I imagine her adjusting her makeup in the rearview mirror, or perhaps sorting through some of the trash she has allowed to engulf the original interior, or crying, in this dangerous moment traveling between two fixed places. Finally, she coasts off. Gerald leaves about forty-five minutes later. I do not hear that as clearly. He does not move the way she does, decisively and purposeful. I sense his departure, the house relaxing, letting down its guard, forgetting about me entirely. I go to the window and see the GTO's invisibility. That, by a natural flow of molecules, rather than any act of will, is how I find myself awake.

I Love You.

Raggedy Ann regards me with her stupid sewn-on smile.

It occurs that I have probably never loved, since I do not seem to value the emotion the way others do. I have longed. I have permitted myself to feel miserable from the lack. But my few romantic encounters were more in the nature of fact-finding expeditions. That is how they seem in retrospect. Concerned not with the nature of the people involved, but explorations of who I was, or what I became, under such extreme circumstances. I have never lost myself, as I hear happens when others deliriously describe "falling in love," as if it were some ritual divestment of personality, revealing a deeper, truer self beneath. But now I do desire to love in that sense. Because maybe I could lose, along with everything else, my cancer, as if it was just another character flaw, leave it behind me, lying on the floor like a dirty shirt.

CHAPTER FIVE

"Say, 'Ah.'"

"Ah."

Macatee pushes the tongue depressor down, hard.

"Again."

I make a choked sound, more an animal's incoherent expression of rage. He does not seem to register the objection, or much of anything else. It is not even clear he has retained his sense of hearing. Nothing I say elicits more than a nod.

"Fever?"

"I get sudden attacks of the shakes. Also night sweats."

"Appetite?"

"Sometimes. Sometimes I throw it back up. But that's getting better. I haven't had an attack in several days."

"All right." He is stooped, a shuffler, with white hair and light hazel eyes that do not seem to take much in. He wears a white coat, just like a doctor on TV, and has a mustache in the shape of a push broom. Yellow streaks spread out from under the nose. I try not to wonder if they are remnants of original color or more recent mudslides of mucous. "You put this on, and I'll be back directly."

"Oh, I don't need that."

It is one of those ridiculous paper gowns.

I hop off the examining table and start removing my clothes.

"Nothing you haven't seen before," I joke.

He seems once again not to have heard, still standing, holding out the flimsy shred of modesty.

All I want is to get this over with.

"I'm stage 3," I try helping the old coot out. "My doctor up North says to sit tight, but I want a bone marrow transplant. So far, I have been unable to find a match."

"Gladys!" he shouts, and takes a few stiff steps to the door. "I'm going to have to ask you to put that gown on."

"If you insist."

I slip into the paper garment, which, paradoxically, makes me colder than I was before. Gladys, the woman out front, doubles as the nurse. I hear him consulting with her in that peculiar mumble some doctors have, turning language into a mode of noncommunication, making everything a mystery.

"Now if you just get up there and put your feet in the stirrups."

"What? A pelvic exam?"

Gladys is standing against the wall, no doubt to contradict any testimony I might give in a molestation trial.

"How's your mamma?" he asks, once I'm spread out.

"Just fine." There is a water stain directly over my head. "Naturally, she's concerned about me."

"Naturally."

"Holy moly!"

"What's that?"

"Nothing."

He must store his speculum in a meat locker. I actually think I am experiencing freezer burns.

"I'm wondering if you know anything about my father," I go on, trying to turn the tables here. "If my mother might have let slip something about his past."

"Your father," he repeats distractedly.

"I just found out neither Mother nor Gerald can be a donor. So I'm hoping to find some collateral relatives."

His only response is another piece of muttered unintelligibility. Gladys gives a knowing, grunting assent, like a congregation egging on its preacher.

"You can get up now."

I relax, inasmuch as that is possible, considering my position.

"Looks like you got some rain damage," I say, just to show I too can play the driveling-on-about-nothing game that passes for social intercourse around here.

His eyes follow to where I am pointing.

"Wind blew the shingles off last winter. I can't get up on the roof no more." He notices I am hugging myself. "Go get yourself dressed."

"No one will tell me," I blurt. I do not want him to leave me in this depressing room. "Someone must have heard something about him. I know this town. People talk. And I *need* to find out."

"You get dressed," he repeats. "We'll discuss it in my office."

He waits, the courtly gentlemen, for Gladys to exit ahead of him. I start putting on my clothes and then, I do not know why, steal a bunch of disposable latex gloves, emptying the box and cramming them into my pants pockets. I have no idea what I will use them for and am not, or have not been, until now, a kleptomaniac, but I want to make him *pay* for what he just did to me, the cold speculum, the colder manner, and cannot think of some super-subtle way to do it.

Besides, subtlety is overrated, I tell myself. Half the time it is just an excuse for doing nothing at all.

When I emerge, Gladys is back at her station.

"Through here?"

65

She nods without looking up, deliberately refusing to address me.

What's your problem? I want to ask. You think I am a strumpet for getting naked in front of the doctor? What do you do? Have him poke around down there from under an afghan?

The office is in the living area of the house. It is a den-like room with vacation photos on the wall. One is of a shipboard group, all of them gathered around the captain's table. Another is a posed hunting portrait, him with a rifle, standing over a just-slaughtered elk. No, wait a minute. I move closer. That turns out to be Mrs. Macatee he is aiming the gun at, in a chair, wearing a fancy hat.

"Have a seat."

"Stage 3," I remind him.

"So I see."

"You have my records?"

"Your doctor sent them. Your mother gave me his address when she made the appointment."

"When was that?"

"A few weeks back."

"Before I was even here?"

"I wouldn't know."

"And he just passed all that along without asking me?"

"You gave your consent. It was one of the forms you signed when you initially asked for a second opinion."

He continues to look over the papers, still reluctant to meet my eyes.

Something wells up in me. I am sick and tired of being made to feel guilty for causing everyone else discomfort! Am I really such a piece of grit in the otherwise smooth working of things? Do I not have enough on my mind without it being implied that I am trespassing on the rest of the world's precious sense of complacency with my direct questions, with my grotesque disease, with my lack of lady-like modesty?

"Everyone wants me to just sit here and see if I get better, but I can't do that. I need to be *cured*. And the only way that is going to happen is through finding out about my daddy." I decide I might as well blast this whole house of cards to smithereens. It is not just the shingles that are going to get blown off, I promise myself. I am taking the whole structure down with me. "Now by virtue of seeing me today, you're my doctor, even though you probably don't want to be. And that means you've got to help me, whether you like it or not. You have my records right there. You see how serious this is. You're not allowed to act like the rest of the people around here and hide behind some wall of Southern gentility and tell me you never heard talk of who he was or where his kin might be located. There's information that I need to know and if you can help me find anything it's your *duty*, medically, legally, and ethically, to do so. You hear?"

He looks up. He is frowning.

Does he know about the gloves? flashes wildly through my mind. Could there be a security camera?

"Kara, your cervix has a light bluish tinge to it."

"Well." I believe the current expression is I *process* that information. It takes a moment. "Your examining room has a draft. I suppose that could account for it. Or maybe it was your equipment. My gynecologist stores hers by a lamp, so it's slightly warm when she uses it. I don't know where you keep yours, probably next to the half gallon of Rocky Road, but—"

"And your vagina is purple."

"What are you, some kind of Sunday painter?"

"It's called Chadwick's sign."

"Who was Chadwick?"

Now it is his turn to look lost. But only for a moment.

"I'd say you're about eight weeks."

I feel for the arms of the chair.

"You mean that's how much time I have left?"

"No. You're eight weeks pregnant. It's plain as day. I could tell from the minute you walked in."

Ah yes. I forgot. He is a "brilliant diagnostician."

"There must be some mistake. That isn't possible."

"You mean you have not been sexually active?"

I am about to say no when a memory overtakes me.

"I don't know if 'active' is the right word. My part in the whole event was quite limited. Besides, it was only a few times, and once he couldn't even—"

"I see you've had both chemotherapy and radiation. Neither of those is recommended during the first trimester. They can lead to premature delivery, birth defects, mental retardation . . . Does your doctor know?"

"My doctor? How could he? I just found out."

"Well, you're going to have to tell him. It could affect your course of treatment."

"I don't *have* a course of treatment. That's why I'm here. To find a bone marrow match."

"I don't know anything about these tales you suspect exist concerning your father. I never met the man. I have known your mother though, ever since she was a little girl. I count her as a friend. And what you're claiming, frankly, that she would keep any kind of information from you, information that might help you in your condition, sounds quite fantastic to me. To be honest, when you talk that way, you sound . . ." He draws the word out of his breast pocket, along with a shiny silver pen. ". . . hysterical."

So that is where we have been heading this whole time. Female hysteria. Which turns out to be seeing Truth, unadorned.

"I'm prescribing prenatal vitamins for you."

"For me?"

"And I want to see you in a month's time, if you're still here."

"For me?" I repeat. "The prenatal vitamins aren't for me, are they?"

"For you and your child."

"I can't have a goddamned child. I'm sick!"

I say it loud enough for Gladys to hear. I can tell she is listening because his eyes stray momentarily to the door. She has probably worn herself a nice little bald patch in the carpet there, over the years.

"Kara," he smiles. It is an utterly insincere expression, too rehearsed to have an atom of genuine feeling behind it. "This isn't the first time I've sat at this desk and told a woman some news she's not prepared to hear. My advice is always the same: Take a deep breath, think about it, and don't come to any rash decisions. After all, we're talking about a human life, here."

"Yes. Mine. How do I get rid of this thing?"

"Federal law does allow termination within the first twelve weeks of pregnancy. But that's something I can't be a party to."

"Well, that's one party I'll have to attend all by myself," I mutter, getting up.

"And though I'm bound to keep this information between ourselves . . ."

"Oh, right," I snort, remembering the birth control incident from tenth grade.

". . . I do urge you to talk to your mother. If you don't feel comfortable confiding in her, try a member of the clergy. They can be surprisingly helpful."

Yes, I think. There's nothing like a closeted gay man to offer advice on affairs of the uterus.

"Don't forget your prescription."

Like a moron, I take it.

"He used a condom," I insist. "At least I think he did. I was busy reading the spines of the books he keeps in his study. There were these floor-to-ceiling shelves. I'd never seen anything like it. They were built right in."

"That is entirely irrelevant," Dr. Vallomthail points out. "We are dealing with a new factor, now. There is no reason to look back. The horse has left the station."

True, I reflect. And you cannot shut the barn door on a speeding train. And Elvis is, disgustingly, *in* the building.

"Why am I always being colonized?"

"Whatever do you mean?"

"First the tumors, and now this. Why am I such fertile ground for alien invasion?"

"I have no idea what you are referring to, Kara. We must focus on your medical options."

"Yes. Of course. Excuse me one moment. Do you mind?"

I glare at the attendant, who is lingering a little too close. He drifts off to run a rag over the front of the gas pumps. A truck roars by, hooting its horn.

"Kara?"

"I'm sorry, doctor. I'm out on the highway."

After getting the news, I walked. Not aimlessly. With a great deal of aim. I walked as far and as fast away from this hellhole of a town as I could manage. And now here I am, at the Pik'n Tote, on the edge of a soybean field.

"Pregnancy can have a very deleterious effect on the immune system. It speeds the progress of the cancer."

"So I've been told. But I had a kind of interesting idea. Is there any way we can cannibalize this baby for parts? Kind of grind him up and extract some of the bone marrow he's already formed? I mean, *he'd* have to be a match, wouldn't he?"

"I am afraid this is not a good connection. I did not quite follow what it was you just said."

Without a cell, I was forced to find a pay phone and call collect. Luckily, Esther still thinks of Arkansas as tin-cup-and-string country. She accepted the charges without even asking why. I feel bad about running up his bill though.

"Dr. Vallomthail, tell me I'm going to be OK!" I wail, as another convoy of diesels pass.

But I cannot hear his answer, and the attendant, who has a face like a fox, keeps looking over, listening so shamelessly that at one point he wipes air, the rag performing circular ministrations to the void.

"—return immediately so we can evaluate your situation."

"Yes," I say, not really listening.

"—cannot be held responsible if you continue to—"

I put the phone down. It is like a drug, the sun, the monoxide, the smell rising off the gasoline-soaked pavement. I am not in possession of my faculties. I am a caterpillar taken over by wasp larvae. Growths, babies . . . I walk toward the Windexed doors.

The Pik'n Tote has everything you could possibly want. Lottery tickets, soda, candy bars, plus all kinds of preassembled food. I buy a sandwich because it is a perfect square, immaculately centered on a Styrofoam plate, sealed off from time by tightly stretched plastic. I do not even notice what kind it is until I take a bite, a perfectly round bite, as if I too embody some kind of ideal, sitting in this field, surrounded by the green-so-green-it-is-almost-black of soy. Chicken salad. My new favorite. I also love the sound the ginger ale can makes, opening. So clean and celebratory. As if it has waited all eternity for this moment. The soil here smells of chemicals, some powerful pesticide they must have laid down, otherwise how could there be no weeds? Like the sandwich, like the lawns on Bluebelle Road, the row expresses perfect geometry. Is that a good thing, making manifest the order Nature is striving toward anyway, or is it Man trying to impose his puritanical will on the messiness of Life?

Chicken salad, it occurs to me, is neither of the words that comprise its name. It is mayonnaise. Ginger ale, too, is not ginger or ale. It is carbonated sugar water. Which brings us to "Kara Bell," no person at all, merely a conveyance vehicle, a delivery system. I take big bites. I gulp. It is the best meal I have had in ages.

Yes, I imagine telling the attendant, I would like to purchase one gallon of your finest gasoline, with which I intend to immolate myself, like a Tibetan monk. Why? Because my body is protesting the presence of Occupying Powers.

"Thank you for coming to get me."

"It was our pleasure," she says, although Shelby, the other half of the implied *we*, spent most of the ride sleeping in his car seat. "You sure you don't want one of these?"

After putting him back upstairs, she has gotten herself an individual bottle of wine cooler from the fridge.

"I had a ginger ale."

"Ooo, lock up your daughters. Kara Bell had a ginger ale."

I told her everything in the car. Everything Macatee told me. She took it with admirable aplomb, even nodding approvingly when I mentioned stealing the latex gloves.

"Serves him right," she said. "The sadist."

"He was a little harsh, springing it on me that way."

"He just likes to fool with people's heads. Don't give him another thought."

We are in the basement of her sumptuous mansion. Martin's toy soldiers have taken over what was once a Ping-Pong table but is now landscaped to represent the scene of the upcoming pageant. Christy very casually plops the cooler smack dab in the middle of her husband's sacred hobby and encourages me to do the same with a box of tissues she has pressed on me, though I am not crying.

"Won't Martin mind us being here?"

"He's not like that. He doesn't do this to get away from me. He'd be tickled pink to see we're taking an interest."

"But we're not. Taking an interest."

"Well, apparently you are. I hear you signed up to be part of that clown show they're putting on at the state park."

"Did I?"

"Figuring on taking potshots at the people we went to school with?"

"I was just trying to be polite."

"Never understood that as a social stratagem." She takes a demure sip, as befits someone drinking at eleven a.m. "So who is it?"

"Who's what?"

"Who's the father?"

"There is no father. There's not going to be a father because there's not going to be a baby."

"Who's the lucky man?"

"It wasn't like that at all. It wasn't even—" I retrieve, for some reason, Gerald's bizarre formulation. "It wasn't even a sexual thing."

She laughs so hard I have to give her the tissues. Chartreuse chardonnay is coming out her nose.

"He's my advisor," I snap. "It grew naturally out of our weekly meetings. It meant nothing. Certainly not to me and I'm sure not to him either."

"What do you mean it grew naturally out of your meetings?"

"He has a rug in his study. A very beautiful rug. Persian."

"And the whole time you were discussing fancy carpeting?"

"He is one of the world's leading experts on analytic philosophy."

"Meaning your vagina."

"It just happened. I didn't mind. I still don't mind, except for the end result."

"Well, it seems to me you should mind. It sounds like sexual harassment. Or even rape."

"I am going to complete my dissertation." I stare at the battlefield, all the soldiers clustered like ants. "I am going to be awarded a

PhD. I am going to receive job offers from major universities. What happens besides that is of very little interest to me. Saul has a brilliant mind."

"Saul?"

"He *pushes* me. He makes me *think*. As long as he does that, I don't care what else he makes me do, which at his age isn't much."

"Wait a minute. How old is this guy?"

"Seventy-five."

"Whoa! That's quite a number. And you knew that, going in?"

"How many dollars does Martin have in his savings account? I'll bet that's quite a number, too. Don't tell me you didn't know it, before you uncrossed your legs. And what are you getting in return? An 'Mrs.' Just another degree. One you're working hard for." The baby is crying again. We both hear, though she is not moving to go get him. "Same as me."

"—not sure it's exactly the same," she says gently, and finishes up her cooler. "I wish you could drink."

"Alcohol doesn't have the same effect on me that it does on you."

"Thank God for that. Otherwise we'd probably both end up in jail."

She reaches all the way across the table, grabs a handful of my shirt, pulls hard, and brings her face about a quarter inch from mine. My hands flutter. They have nowhere to go. The gap is too far to reciprocate or to make her stop, even if they could decide which of those two is what they want. I taste wine.

"Seventy-five," she mocks, holding me hostage. "What does he do? Make you feel like you're his special little girl?"

That would be you, I want to say. That would be you, who does that.

"Damn."

She cocks her head. Shelby's cries are louder, more outraged.

"It's like I'm a dog responding to a whistle the rest of the human race gets to ignore," she complains, heading for the stairs.

I am still bent awkwardly over the table, speechless, as usual.

"You know what your problem is?" She pauses at the top step and looks down. "You're terrified of being normal."

"I am not."

"Yes, you are. You look at your mother, and she freaks you out so much you do everything you can to run in the opposite direction."

"You saying I'm like her?"

"I'm saying that wouldn't be the end of the world. She's kind of cool, actually. She did a good job raising you and Gerald all on her own. You look down your nose at her—and at people like me, don't deny it—but from where? From where have you got to, Miss 185 IQ? Lying on some old goat's carpet while he instructs you in fellatio-ology or whatever it's called."

"Epistemology. It's the study of knowledge."

"Oh, excuse me. Speaking of knowledge, I have to go and ream some crap out of my son's asshole right now. You stay down here and solve the mystery of existence."

I lower myself until the battlefield is at eye level. The soldiers are careful reproductions, uniforms and weapons and ranks meticulously rendered. They must be custom-made. Their faces though are all the same. Mustachioed youth. Basically, they are clones. Some are lying on the ground, aiming their rifle. Others are charging, bayonet at the ready. There is a sniper in a tree, a man next to a toy canon. Hundreds of them with the same face but poured into different poses, which they must now maintain, for life.

"Isn't it early?"

"Early?" Christy laughs. "Since when is six o'clock in the evening early?"

Martin takes up her tone, even though he must know what I mean.

"—folks still asleep in New York City?"

"I meant early in the summer."

"Oh no, Kara. This is traditional. I'm surprised you don't remember."

We are in Martin's fancy foreign car. An Audi or a Volvo. Something safe. They are up front. Ilene is home with Shelby.

"But school just got out. How can they have a team when—?"

"Who needs school?" she scoffs. "These boys are not what you would call Road Scholars."

"You OK back there?"

Martin is more solicitous. He even offered me an extra Witch's Falls football jersey, which I politely refused, in addition to much other embarrassing regalia. They are completely decked out. It looks good on them. "You can't go like that," Christy had said. Finally I consented to have a pennant featuring the mascot, a crazed pterodactyl, thrust into my unwilling fist.

"It's a way to get familiar with the new players," she explains. "And raise money for the team."

"You once turned down a position on the cheerleading squad. Don't you remember?"

"It's also an excellent opportunity for Martin to meet and greet."

"Touch base with clients," he elaborates.

"Are we any good?"

"Our coach is an offensive genius."

"That's what I always wanted to be."

"Well, there's still time, honey." Christy turns in her seat and takes my hand. "Although you never showed much aptitude for athletics, as I recall."

"Kara is an athlete of the mind," Martin admires.

"She was always a little shy in the locker room."

The entire population has converged on the field, renamed The Eagles Nest. We used to be the Warlocks, which made sense, considering the name of the town, but then a faction claimed that made us appear to be Satan worshippers. The Sorcerers was proposed as an alternative, but people found it too difficult to spell or even pronounce, so they finally settled on the Screaming Eagles, for precisely no reason at all.

There is not a game, it turns out, just a bunch of boys muffled in shoulder pads and helmets doing calisthenics and various drills while girls in costumes whip the crowd into a frenzy. I drift through it all, mercifully invisible. A man with a bullhorn hectors us with bromides. There is a hot dog truck, a soft-serve ice cream machine, and a stand offering many more opportunities to stock up on paraphernalia. An army of students has been pressed into service selling raffle tickets. One for a dollar, fifteen for ten.

"What's the big prize?" I ask.

"Speedboat," a youth with spectacular acne answers.

He scowls at my four quarters, as if they are a suspect form of currency.

"Think I'll win?"

"Thank you, sir," he mumbles, moving on.

Sir!

I run a palm over my fuzz. So I have progressed, in my slow recovery, from asexual freak to incompetent female impersonator.

Groups of former classmates pass, some of them, with their group-eye, tentatively acknowledging me, but more as a dream sighting (Oh yes, I heard she was back in town) than reason to engage in conversation. I am still holding the pennant, a little flag on a stick. I would like to throw it in a trash basket but am afraid that might cause a riot, like burning a Koran.

"And here he is, Coach Kip!"

The man tries handing the bullhorn over to a heavyset specimen with clenched jaw and vain, combed-over hair who has trotted onto the green plastic field. But Coach Kip waves it aside. He does not need artificial enhancements.

"I'd like to thank you all for coming," he booms. "This marks the start of what I guarantee will be an epoch-making season."

Offensive, I agree, noting how he stands with hands on hips, arrogantly thrusting his gut toward the crowd. Not so sure about the genius part.

"You know," he continues folksily, "Plato said the world we see is shadows, shadows cast by Forms. Now I intend to lead these fine young men out of the cave that they have been dwelling in, out into the light, and *smash* those Forms, those idols, that have kept us in the dark for so long!"

I blink.

In fact, he has said nothing of the sort. He is blaring on about "community values."

You need to get out of the sun, girl, I advise.

My feet lead me around to the side, so I can go under the bleachers. But before I escape the acute, slicing rays that are causing my synapses to implode, I catch a glimpse of Gerald, in the stands, talking to a girl I have never seen before. At first glance, she is not his type, meaning I cannot picture her ankles waving like a bug's feelers above the twin headrests of the GTO. She is dressed simply in a navy blouse and what Mother would call Sears work pants even though there has not been a Sears around here in ages. Her hair is tied back in a severe ponytail. She wears dark glasses and seems intent on the game, or the pep talk, rather. Gerald is speaking to her with a strange urgency, very unlike his usual laid-back attitude. She, however, does not seem to be responding, or to even acknowledge his presence.

"The pre-Socratics, with their emphasis on Love and Strife as the sole agents of change, may have been on to something . . ."

I slip into the smelly shade and wait for my eyes, ears, and psyche to recover.

The crowd bursts into applause, then rhythmic foot stomping that, down here, makes the very air shake. I move to the back, where a bunch of kids are concealed. They are familiar types, outcasts, huddled together for protection. A joint is being passed.

"Howdy," I say.

They do not know who I am, but my physical appearance grants me entrée to their pseudo-nonconformist circle. The boys, despite token attempts at outrageousness, are so runtish-looking I assume it is an act, that they would be out there doing jumping jacks if they could. The girls are more problematic. One of them has razor-blade earrings and a giant safety pin stuck through her nose. The other is more retiring, with an angel face, and wears, in the summer heat, heavy-duty construction boots . . . with the toes cut out, I note admiringly.

"This is like journeying through the Underworld." My thoughts express themselves as sculptures of green smoke. "I mean, look up."

"Just a bunch of butts," one of the boys snickers.

"No. We are beneath it all. You have to picture yourself as Orpheus, descending into Hades to rescue his wife. Charming the gods with his lyre playing and then leading her out. Or trying to. Of course, we all know how that ended."

The girl with the razor blades and safety pin is staring at me.

"It's a myth," I reassure her. "A Greek myth. One could argue he is really trying to rescue himself."

Could one?

". . . from his fascination with death and dying."

"Are you Coach's daughter?" she asks.

"No. Why do you think that?"

"They say he's got a daughter. In Chicago."

"I am no man's daughter, apparently. And certainly not from Chicago."

"You talk funny," the girl featuring the psycho footwear elaborates, not in an unfriendly way. "Are you from up North?"

"Don't be silly. I'm from Witch's Falls."

They greet this claim with a dubious silence.

"It's true, I've been away. But I don't think it has affected my speech. Everyone in New York says I talk like I'm from down here."

"What's he like?"

"Who?"

"Coach Kip."

"How should I know?"

"You're not his daughter?"

"No. And I am not from Chicago, either." I try to clear up all the misunderstandings with a blanket statement: "Whoever you think I am, I am not."

I do not exist within the severely limited scope of your collective mind, is what I am really trying to convey.

What is wrong with being terrified of normal? my stoned consciousness finally answers Christy's accusation, hours too late. Normal is all right when it catches up with you. It always does, in the end. But I do not see the point in running *toward* normal. I do not see the point in embracing middle-aged mediocrity like it is your long-lost love.

"I like your boots," I tell the girl.

"They're kind of like sandals."

"I can see that."

"But with protection."

"Yes."

Soon, you won't need any of that, I want to let her know. Soon you will be weird all on your own. Nature will mark you out for scapegoating without any effort on your part. Look at me.

I try and tell them about the Orpheus myth, though the more I go on the more I realize it is a losing proposition.

"So you're Greek," one of the boys confirms.

There is no game, but the announcer somehow manages to declare it "halftime." I emerge from the back of the stands, dragging my pennant, just as the marching band starts up. Trumpets crack a million notes, limping after the elusive beat. Segregation is pretty much still in effect, here. Ours is the largely white high school, and a certain amount of pride is taken in just how badly we play. No Nubian syncopation for us. I see, across the parking lot, Gerald's GTO. Alongside it, Gerald himself is still engaged in a life-or-death discussion with the same woman as before. I have never seen him so earnest. Yet it is not a steamy encounter. He is not touching her, and she, still behind dark glasses, is showing no emotion at all, just waiting expectantly as if listening to birdcalls or distant thunder. I am embarrassed to have stumbled upon this moment, but there is no place to go, nothing to hide behind. Finally, she answers, in just a few words. Her face is expressionless. He seems to accept whatever it is she says, then takes her upper arm, and starts helping her into the front seat. That is when I realize she is blind.

CHAPTER SIX

I try thinking things through at the counter of Kreski's, our local luncheonette. Sometimes it helps to have a low-level murmur in the background. I am hoping that by placing myself between a discussion of hysterectomies ("They took something out of her big as a grapefruit!") and what threatens to become a physical altercation concerning steel-belted radial tires, I will be able to arrive at an appropriate course of action. What I really need is a push. I should be calling clinics, figuring a way to scrape together money, arranging for transportation . . . Frankly though, considering my circumstances, all that seems laughable. I pour sugar in my coffee and do not bother to stop, marveling at how the white waterfall dissolves in the sludgy brown liquid without raising the level one bit. It dispels the laws of physics and so invalidates, in advance, any attempt I might make to employ logic in solving my problems.

"Sweet tooth?" the woman next to me asks.

She smiles like we know each other.

"Mrs. Dawes." She waits, then adds, "Gladys."

"Oh."

Just when I think the two men on my other side are about to start a brawl over Firestone versus Goodyear, they laugh uproariously and slap each other on the back. I do not understand male conversation. It seems more a method of farting-out-the-mouth.

"You left awful fast, the other day."

"I was in a rush."

"I'd've been, too."

I look at her. She is a short woman, in her fifties, not as reflexively censorious as I remember. She has kind eyes.

Kind of prying, I warn myself.

She is eating pie.

"Doc gets worked up sometimes. You can't take him too serious."

"How long have you been there?"

"Oh my. Going on twenty years, at least."

"Is he going to tell my mamma?"

"He might," she admits. "Of course, he shouldn't, legally. You're of age, aren't you?"

"I'm twenty-three!"

"You still look so young. I have five, myself."

"It's the no-hair." I force myself to take a sickeningly sweet sip. "That throws people off, age-wise."

I hesitate to drink more. She sees my dilemma.

"Candy," she calls. "Could I have a cup of coffee, please?"

For some reason, the waitress regards this as a major news event.

"You never drink coffee."

"I'm feeling a little tired."

"Since when?"

"I don't know since when. Maybe I didn't sleep well last night. Maybe I had bad dreams."

Totally not buying it, acting like she is being forced to participate in a criminal enterprise, Candy pours a cup. As soon as the girl's back is turned, we switch.

"Thank you."

"It's not the hair," she resumes. "It's you. You're still young, even if you don't feel it."

"I don't want my mother to know about this."

"She's going to, eventually."

"Oh no she's not."

"I'd think twice before I did anything, if I were you. It's a life. You don't want that weighing on your conscience."

"Is it? A life?" I warm to the argument, as I would in a seminar, where I am known, believe it or not, for being dangerous, for being someone not to mess with. "You think a fetus in the womb is a living being? With legal rights?"

She looks both ways, but now there is a long, arcane disquisition being delivered upon the 1995 Razorbacks Basketball Team, Exactly Where Did They Go Wrong?

"If that's so, then we are all nine months older than we claim. Drinking and voting ages would have to be revised, for starters. Horoscopes would need to be redrawn. You see, you want to let the lawyers in, to prove your point, but once you let them in they're not going to leave so easily. Once you start using the penal code to enforce religion it might take you places you don't want to go."

"No point in arguing belief," she smiles.

"On the contrary, that is what one should argue. One should examine one's positions. To whit—"

"To what?"

"—Abortion Should Be Illegal Because Life Begins at Conception, is that your proposition? And you are basing this on religious, not medical grounds, correct? Because most doctors would disagree with you. Well, fine. Then when does life end? With the stopping of the heart? I think not. Not if we are using Christianity as our guide. Jesus conquered death, didn't He? Romans 6:9." Now it is my turn to look about, see if anyone is willing to contradict me. "So we don't really die, if we are letting religion dictate the law of the land. If we are taking the Bible *fundamentally*. Ergo, with no death we have no distribution of wealth, no inheritance."

"I don't think—"

"That means they should keep paying taxes, shouldn't they? The so-called dead? Until the time of Revelation. And don't even get me started on second marriages, since couples will be reunited, won't they? Thessalonians 4:16. Matthew 18:18. So there go the rights of not just divorced people but widows and widowers, too. It's one and done. You see what absurd lengths this can be taken to?"

"He might tell your mamma," she resumes, treating my finely crafted position as she would the combined babblings of her five wet-mouthed offspring, "if he feels you're not facing up to it. If he feels you're mentally incompetent."

"Incompetent!"

"How's that coffee?" Candy asks suspiciously.

She raises her cup, takes a sip, and doesn't bat an eye.

"I'm competent," I hiss, once the coast is clear again. "Competent enough to slap a malpractice suit on that joker if he—"

"You should tell him you're going to a priest," she decides. "That'd do it."

"Do what?"

"Stop him from telling. Didn't he give you that line about consulting a member of the clergy? He usually does."

"Yes."

"Well, you and your mamma go to Saint Archibald's. So tell him you're talking to the priest there. Then he'll feel his responsibility is at an end."

"I'm not telling him anything. I'm not going near that man ever again. He's a menace." I shift uncomfortably on my seat, as if his ice-cold speculum is gunning to make a repeat performance. "Can't *you* tell him? Say we ran into each other here? That we got to talking, and that's what I said I'd do?"

She hesitates.

"It would mean a lot to me. I just couldn't bear to have my mother find out now. On top of everything else she's had to put up with, in terms of my health. She's pretty close to the breaking point, as it is."

"Well, will you?" she asks.

"Will I what?"

"Talk to a member of the clergy about this? I can't tell the doctor something if it's not true."

I look into her kind eyes.

"Yes. I will. I promise."

"All right, then. I'll let him know. That should give you enough time to make your decision in peace."

"Five kids." I shake my head, imagining. "I guess you never got one."

"Got one what?"

"A procedure."

"Certainly not!" She is about to act righteous but then changes her mind. "I did think about it once. With my last."

"And?"

"Well, now of course I'm very glad I didn't. But at the time . . ."

The conversation around us has ebbed, so we have to murmur.

"Thank you," I whisper. "I feel if this became public knowledge everyone here would tear me limb from limb."

"That's not true," she frowns, and makes a gesture allying herself with all the occupants of the counter, not to mention those at the tables. "We're good people."

"So the trooper gets out. The inside of my car is totally fogged up. He takes the butt of his flashlight and goes *narc narc narc* on the window. Scares the hell out of us. Lonmell is trying to pull up his pants. I wait a bit, then—"

"Lonmell?"

"Lonmell Richardson. You don't know him."

"What kind of name is that?"

"Just a name. Anyway, Lonmell is—"

"Sure you don't want to join me?"

We are on the roof, A.C. and me. He told me he felt bad about the weed I bought, said there were issues with "quality control," and came by with better stuff. I appreciate that, but am disappointed to have him, once again, only watch. Instead of smoking, he jabbers away, a mile a minute.

"I don't mix," he explains.

"Mix what with what?"

"So Lonmell—"

"What are you doing instead, that you don't want to mix it with?"

"Nothing."

"You doing crystal?"

"Nobody calls it that anymore."

"Shit, A.C. You shouldn't be doing crystal."

"You shouldn't be wearing purple with . . ." He squints in the late evening dusk. ". . . orange?"

"It's just a shirt."

"When are you going to finally figure out that nothing is just a shirt?"

"You shouldn't be doing that," I repeat.

"I'm not. Not in any kind of serious way. It's just part of the scene, these days. You got to go along to get along. You have no idea what it's like. Everything's different than when we were growing up. You're still in a cocoon."

"Is that what this is?"

"Anyway, just when he's about to search the car, he gets a call on his radio, Burglary in progress or something, and has to go. Runs off. Otherwise—"

"You got any?"

"Got any what?"

"Whatever it is you call it now. You got any on you?"

He looks around. There is no one else here. We are on an island of tar approximately the size of a picnic bench.

"You don't want to be doing none of this, Kara."

"Meth? Why not? I hear it helps you focus."

"That's the last thing you need. You focus so hard you set things on fire."

"I miss you." I take one of his lovely hands. "I miss doing stuff together, like we used to."

"All we ever did together was have us a pity party."

"What's wrong with that? Isn't that pretty much the definition of friendship?"

"I got things on my mind."

"What things?"

"Well, for one, trying not to end up like my dog."

"Me too." I put out the joint. "Now give me some of that shit or I'll push you off the roof."

"It wouldn't be right."

"Albert Claude Evans," I threaten, "do I have to remind you of all the papers I wrote in your name, the tests I helped you pass, the *eyeliner* you had me buy because you were too embarrassed to walk into Cunningham's Drug and ask for it yourself?"

"All right, all right. She's so bossy," he complains to an invisible third party, digging into his pocket. "Don't know why I put up with her."

"This Lonmell. Is it serious?"

"Why? You jealous?"

"Maybe. He have a sister?"

I am surprised to see it is in glass, a glass pipe. I really have no idea what I am doing, what I am asking. I feel goofy. Also scared.

"I'm giving you one hit and then I'm cutting you off for the rest of your natural life, understand?"

"Sounds fair."

I do it, and it's no big deal. "Focus" isn't really the right word, though. It is more like the molecules composing the surrounding world become tighter, more packed together, like the surface of a trampoline. Everything firms up. I, however, remain unaffected.

"You might want to breathe," A.C. suggests.

The door below us opens and Gerald walks out. Viewed from directly overhead, he seems to float. Despite the lack of light, I notice how organized his scalp is, each strand of hair with a specific purpose, individuated as a thumbprint.

"You like my brother?"

"I like his car."

We watch as he gets into the GTO.

"Let's follow him."

"Follow him where?"

"How should I know? That's the point. Follow him to see where he goes."

"He's going nowhere."

"No. He's been doing this almost every night." I am already straddling the windowsill, climbing back in. "He's up to something. I can tell."

"What business is it of yours?"

"It'll give us something to do. Come on!"

"So bossy," he whines again.

I resist the urge to swoop, like a flying squirrel, from the top step of the staircase. The knob at the bottom of the bannister, which dragged me down like a magnet when I first arrived, acts now as a charging station. I swing around it and shoot off with renewed purpose, only to be clobbered by a door that refuses to open.

"Pull, don't push," A.C. calls.

"It wasn't responding properly."

"Uh-huh."

In the car, I grip the sides of the seat as if we are going a hundred miles an hour.

"He's heading for the highway," I mutter. "What does that *mean?*"

"It means gasoline. How much is this going to cost me?"

"Keep back. We don't want him to spot us."

"Spot us doing what? I don't even know why we're here."

"Better than sitting on the roof."

I watch the tall reeds of the entrance ramp flash by, feel the irrational exuberance of leaving, however briefly.

"Gerald Bell," A.C. sighs, settling in behind him.

"Can't you go any faster?"

"First you tell me to slow down, then you tell me to speed up. That stuff got right inside you, didn't it?"

"Are you attracted to my brother?"

"What?"

"You heard me."

"He's *young.*"

"That was in high school. Who cares about that now? Don't you think he's beautiful?"

"He is a white boy."

"And white boys can't be beautiful?"

"They can be. They *can* be," he reemphasizes, obviously remembering an incident. "But it's childish, going for boys like that."

"Why?"

I feel like pouncing on every word he says. Even before they leave his mouth. It occurs to me that I know what people are going to say, ninety-nine percent of the time.

"Why childish?"

. . . whereas I never know what I am going to say until I have said it. Is that normal?

"It's just a crush-type thing. Not real. Like that Miss America you used to run after."

91

"Who? Who do you mean?"

"Chrissy?"

"Christy. Christy Lee."

"Yeah. Barbie doll."

"She's not a Barbie doll."

"She might as well be. That's not real."

"You don't think a crush is real? You don't think that it's a legitimate emotion?"

"I don't know."

"Or you don't think that my version of her exists? You don't think that the 'she' I imagine is real. Is that what you mean?"

"You're getting me confused."

"I am trying to get you to clarify your terms!"

"—knew I shouldn't have given you that shit. It just makes you more you."

"And another thing: Do I talk funny?"

He laughs.

"No, I'm serious. I was hanging out with these girls under the bleachers—"

"I'll bet you were."

"—and one of them said I talked like I wasn't from around here. Like I was from up North. Do you think that's true? Do you think I've acquired an accent?"

"Do I think you have an acquired an accent?" he mimics.

I hit him. The car almost goes off the road.

"Stop that!" he screams. "I cannot afford another police incident."

"OK, OK. Sorry."

"You *always* talked funny."

"I speak correctly," I say, making a great effort to do so. "That is different from sounding like I am from somewhere I am not."

"I imagine up there you sound like you're from down here, and down here you sound like you're from up there."

"I do?"

Immediately, he tries to make amends.

"A little. I don't know. I don't even *listen* to what you say, Kara. Not like that. You're just . . ." He waves his hand at an elusive concept. ". . . crickets."

"Oh, well thank you very much."

"You know what I mean. You're nighttime and riding around and us waiting to grow up and stuff. I never paid much attention to the actual words."

I cannot decide if that is a compliment or not.

"Looks like he's getting off at Booneville. What the hell's in Booneville?"

"Christy Lee is Christine Casimir, now," I sigh.

"Yeah. And here you are giving me grief over 'Lonmell.'"

"Is that a love-type situation, you and him?"

He snorts.

"I don't hear you saying no."

"He's a nice guy."

"Where'd you meet?"

"I don't want to get into all that."

"Must be serious."

"It is on my part," he says simply. "So Gerald's two-timing that honey who hangs out at the parlor? Doesn't sound like him."

"No. It doesn't. That's why I'm concerned. Not that Delilah Samson is going to win the Nobel Prize for Consecutive Reasoning, but still . . ."

"I'm waiting for the part that has anything to do with us being here."

"How come you're so grouchy these days?" I complain. "You used to be up for just this kind of thing. Manufacturing adventure when there was none around. Driving through the night. That was what we did best."

93

"Driving through the night costs. Everything costs."

"I thought your business pretty much took care of that."

"What business? It's like I've been trying to tell you, I'm getting muscled out. Losing my connections. That's why I could only find you bad shit the other day."

I sigh.

I was going to tell him about my need for the procedure, maybe even ask for a loan, but now I see he might even be worse off than me, if such a thing is possible.

"So much for adventure," A.C. sighs.

Gerald is not going to Booneville. We pull into a newly paved parking lot. A huge sign, angled so it can be read from the highway, towers over a nondescript building. I, by contrast, get very excited.

"The Best!"

"Shh!"

We both slump as Gerald, getting out of the car, looks over.

"The Best Steakhouse in Booneville!" I whisper from beneath the dashboard.

"I know what it is. Cracker hangout. No way I'm going in there."

"Sure you are. We'll split an order of fries."

"In a parallel universe, maybe."

"They're not going to think we're on a date."

"You'd be surprised at how dumb these people are."

"No, I wouldn't. I'm one of them, remember?"

"I can't go in there," he repeats. "I'm not dressed for it."

The light from the sign is strong enough for me to evaluate his shirt. It is a painfully bright shade of canary, the usual several sizes too small, reading, *Nobody Calls Me Yellow*.

"I see your point."

"Come on. We'll go somewhere else. Talk about our problems. Just like old times."

"I can't," I declare. "I've got to go in there and nip this thing in the bud."

"Why?"

"Don't you see? He's cheating on Delilah Samson with some *other* moron."

"What do you care?"

"He's my baby brother. I don't want to see him committing an ethical violation."

"Sounds like you're paying a lot of attention to everyone else's flaws but not much to your own."

I slam the door.

"Hold on a sec," he calls. "How you going to get back?"

"I'll get a ride from Gerald."

"He's not going to want you there."

"Nobody wants me anywhere," I answer haughtily. "But that does not stop me from going."

"Kara, wait!"

I am beyond determined. I march across the white lines of the parking lot.

The Best is one of those pillbox establishments, more cinder block than glass, but inside all pretend-antique lamps and carpeting. I linger before the second set of doors, trying to find him in the row of booths lining one wall. There is a stuffed bison in the middle of the room and the smell of—somehow you can tell—tough meat coming from the kitchen. The hostess sees me and waves, pretty much forcing me to come on in.

"How-you-all-doing?" she recites. "Welcome to The Best Steakhouse in Booneville."

"I'm looking for someone," I say, craning my neck.

There are a few couples and several families, but no Gerald.

"Is he at the meeting?"

"What meeting?"

"That's in the Chickasaw Room."

She leads me toward a partially drawn curtain. I can feel my resolve weakening with each step. It is easy to playact in front of A.C. Confronting the cud-chewing patrons of a chain restaurant steakhouse is harder.

"There's quite a turnout tonight."

"Turnout for what?"

She steps aside, and I walk through.

Gerald is sitting next to the woman I saw before, the blind girl in the parking lot, at a long table. It is the kind of room where they hold banquets or business luncheons. There is some lame attempt at an Indian theme, with wigwams printed right onto the wallpaper.

"Hello," the girl calls, sensing my arrival. "Welcome."

She is younger than I thought, maybe twenty. Not wearing cosmetics or jewelry makes her look older, almost middle-aged, in a fresh-faced way. Her dark glasses, indoors, reflect the lights overhead and redirect them, so she seems to glint at me. I try not to make eye contact with Gerald.

"I'm Amy."

"Kara."

The rest look like a bunch of people who have been caught in some shameful act, a bunch of embarrassed victims.

"Have a seat, Kara."

There are chairs available along the sides, but since she is at one end, I take the other. The head and the foot of the table. It has never been clear to me which is which. I suppose it depends on who is doing the sitting.

The others go around and introduce themselves. I do not know any of them. They are mostly from Booneville, I assume. When it comes to Gerald, he levels his howitzer of a blank stare at me.

"Pleased to meet you," I grin.

"She doesn't have a book," someone notes.

"Gerald."

That is all she has to say. He is her right-hand man. He gets up, retrieves a leatherette volume from a box along the wall, and places it before me.

"Here you go."

"Much obliged."

I take a look and almost hoot out loud. It is the Book of Mormon, complete with cheesy Technicolor illustrations of Joseph Smith, Brigham Young, and, of course, the Angel Moroni.

"We were just discussing the LDS's relationship with our Native American brothers and sisters. The LDS believes—"

"Excuse me," I interrupt. "Are you on your mission year?"

"That's right." Her face is strangely immobile. "I am based in our Little Rock Outreach Center but come here once a week to lead this group for those interested in conversion."

"All the way from Little Rock? How do you get here?"

"—not really important," Gerald warns.

"No, that's all right."

She touches his forearm. How did she know it was there? They seem to have some kind of bond.

"I take a bus, and then Alan . . ." she nods to one of the other expectant dorks, they all wear those embarrassing stick-on nametags, " kindly meets me and drives me here."

"How did you come to find us, Kara?" someone else asks.

"Me? I'm going through a crisis of faith."

"I can sense that," Amy nods, still without any inflection or empathy. "I sensed that the minute you walked in. Are you ill?"

"Not really."

"She has cancer," Gerald says.

"Of course." Her eyes, even though I know it is not really possible, seem to zero in on me from behind those dark glasses. Just for an instant. Then, without missing a beat, she explains, "The LDS believes that Native Americans are, in fact, the descendants of the Jenites, one of the Lost Tribes of Israel . . ."

"How dare you?"

"How dare I what?"

"Tell them that I was sick."

"I didn't have to tell them. They could see it for themselves, what with your hair and stuff. It's still pretty obvious."

"But she couldn't."

"Exactly. And I didn't want her to be at a disadvantage."

"Oh, well, aren't you her knight in shining armor? What did you do to get that guy Alan to bow out of the picture? Threaten him with violence?"

"He works security at one of the plants. Midnight to eight. He picks her up, and I drop her off. I can't believe *you're* mad at *me*."

We are waiting outside the ladies room while Amy does her business. The rest of the group has already taken their leave. Several of the women hugged me. One whispered "God bless" in my ear. I am reduced to standing with Gerald, both of us holding our booby prize gospels. His, I can't help but notice, has actual handwritten notes in the margins.

". . . following me, barging in like that. What gives you the right?"

"Because I thought you were fooling around with another woman."

He snorts, but does not deny it.

"I wish I *had* caught you with your pants down. That would be much less of a betrayal than this."

"You don't know nothing about it."

"I know that for a formerly cool dude you're considering joining one of the dullest cults in all of Christendom."

"There's more to life than being cool. And what you call dumb . . ."

We step aside while someone else leaves. She is taking forever in there.

"What I call 'dumb' is what?"

"Never mind."

". . . is the Truth? As delivered from on high in the form of gold printing plates which then mysteriously disappeared?"

"I feel something." He turns to me with a pained look and points to his chest. "I feel it right here. Has that ever happened to you? Have you ever just known something is true?"

"Of course not. To know something is true without proving it is to misapply the concept. Truth is arrived at. It is demonstrated. You see it."

"What if you're blind?"

"Kara?" Amy calls.

". . . then you couldn't go looking for Truth that way, could you? You'd have to *accept* it."

"I wonder if you could come in here for a minute? I need a little help."

"Sure thing," I answer, but, before I can move, Gerald grabs me.

He is the most gentle man I know, which makes the force with which he grips my shoulders all the more shocking.

"Be nice or I will kill you," he instructs.

"I just don't want to see you making a big mistake."

"It's mine to make."

He lets go, but I can feel the marks he leaves.

She is squatting in front of the sinks. Her bag has spilled open. Most of the stuff is swept into a little pile, but a few things are beyond her reach. ChapStick. A change purse.

"Everything goes in a specific place," she explains. "Could you hand them to me one by one, so I can organize?"

I kneel next to her on the floor. I am intrigued by her face, its lack, not just of expression, but how it does not give anything away. You cannot say if she is pretty or ugly, young or old, male or female even.

"I'm very glad you came."

"That's OK. Anybody would have helped."

"I mean to our meeting."

"Oh, well, that was more by accident. I just kind of wandered in."

"Accidents are often the workings of God in disguise."

I hand her each object. She feels, identifies, and sorts accordingly.

"Gerald seems pretty serious about all this."

"He has a very wide spiritual streak."

"That makes him sound like a skunk."

Then I think, She has never even seen a skunk. Or anything.

"He's a good man."

"He likes you," I say.

We stand up. She is dressed badly. As badly as I am, but in a different way, favoring lackluster beiges I would not inflict on waiting room furniture. To hide stains, I decide. I remember reading how blind people drop a lot of food. Her shoes though are surprisingly stylish.

"There's a special bond that develops when you are privileged to introduce a newcomer to the Word."

"I'll bet."

"Maybe you and I will get to experience that too."

"You never know."

I try guiding her out. She rather brusquely sets me aside.

"I know my way," she says.

In the car, I insist on her sitting up front.

"You guys probably have a lot more to talk about."

But we ride in silence. There is a first-date awkwardness between them. I am itching to ask about polygamy, all those women living in the same house with one token male. Don't tell me there are not nights of outrageous hanky-panky. But something holds me back. Her seriousness. No doubt that is what Gerald responds to. She starts talking about "living ordinances," some zany master plan to retroactively baptize every person who has ever lived on Earth during the entire history of recorded time.

"Why?" I ask, not even trying to suppress a note of derisive incredulity.

"So they can enter heaven." It is a catechism she has learned, a bright flimsy singsong with no thought behind it. "That's why the LDS has its Archive Department, which keeps extensive records of births and deaths going back over three centuries."

"Wait a minute." I lean forward, sticking my head between them like the family dog. "You mean for Gerald to convert, he'd have to find out where he came from?"

"Conversion is a process, not an event. But yes, one of the living ordinances is baptizing not just the person entering the church, but his ancestors as well."

"So he'd have to construct a family tree."

"Kara," Gerald drawls, "if I come to a sudden stop you're going to go right through the windshield."

"And how does he do that? Where does he go?"

"It'd be like you were shot out of a cannon."

"There's a Family History Center in Utah. They can track down almost anyone's past."

"Can they?"

". . . probably fracture every bone in your body."

"We haven't talked about your illness," she says.

"I'm fine, thanks."

"I hope you are. But surely you must have wondered what happens when you die. Where you'll go."

"No," I answer truthfully. "Never for one second."

"Kara only believes in the here-and-now," he announces, with a certain amount of pride.

I smile.

"Well, that can't be." Her hands are securely folded over that bag, with its pockets and compartments. "If that's true, why did you come to our meeting tonight?"

"Sure wasn't for the rib eye."

"They do a good garden salad," Gerald says. "You should try the blue cheese dressing."

"I wish you had told me that earlier."

"I didn't feel we knew each other well enough," he answers lightly. "Remember, we just met."

"We should continue this conversation, Kara." She means alone. "Some other time."

CHAPTER SEVEN

"If you'll all just take your seats."

I had thought coming back to my high school auditorium would be strange, but it is just a dinky, rundown hall. I sit where I used to at assemblies, all the way in back. Martin, who, as I said before, was pretty much a nonentity, growing up, now dominates the room. You can tell, as he stands behind the lectern, his voice fading in and out of the tinny microphone's range, that he has money. It gives his words a kind of emphasis, invisible italics, that have nothing to do with their actual sense. "Maneuvers will commence at 0630," inspires the awestruck hush of several million dollars making its wishes known.

I do not know why I am here. I do not know why I even consented—indeed, I do not remember consenting—to take part in this stupid military "pageant," but that is the essence of small town life. Currents sweep you along. All you try to do is stay afloat, keep your head above water, then look down one day and find yourself (I survey my fellow soldiers) prematurely aged and child-ridden, all from "doing what is right," which turns out not to be right at all, not to even be doing, just going along, allowing expectations to have their way.

My stomach twitches.

That was not a kick, I assure myself. It is far too early for that.

It happens again.

Psychosomatic.

Without thinking, I punch myself in the gut. Hard.

"I wish he had worn his other tie."

Ilene Casimir slides in place beside me. She exudes a very subtle scent. Not perfume. Maybe body wash? Maybe it is just, like the importance Martin's innocuous instructions put out, money. I see her emerging from the shower and applying hundred dollar bills like deodorant.

"I had one made with our family crest, but he never wears it."

"I think he looks good."

"Of course he does." She sits back contentedly, not self-conscious about the seat creaking. "I'm so glad you came, Kara."

"I wouldn't have missed it for the world."

"Christy makes fun of him for this, but I think it's important to remember our roots."

For you, would that not involve dressing in the native garb of Cracow, Poland? I toy with asking, but instead opt for:

"She probably got enough of that growing up, being named Lee and all."

"I hardly think she's a *descendant*," Ilene frowns, unable to take her eyes off Martin.

"No. But if you're born here you get a fair amount of that 'the South will rise again' stuff from early on. It can get tiresome."

"Martin was born here."

"Yes, he was."

"Now the room," he says, "looks pretty evenly divided as you're sitting. So let's say the people on the left, my left, will be the Union forces, and those on the right, my right, the soldiers of the Confederacy. Your uniform will be provided several days before the—"

104

"Wait!" I call, not fully realizing what I am doing. "I don't want to be no Union soldier."

There are a few titters from the crowd, but I do not care. I feel my legitimacy is being attacked.

"None of us want to be a Union soldier," Martin smiles, getting even more of a laugh. "But someone's got to do it."

"You been up there," Mr. Albertson, who runs the hardware store, points out. "It'd be more realistic."

"I am not portraying a Union soldier," I declare flatly.

I seem to be standing.

"We can discuss this later, Kara."

"You could make a speech about being on the right side," a woman, some frenemy of Mother's, no doubt, suggests sarcastically.

I realize I am making a fool of myself, but I do not care. In fact, it excites me. It is when you are making a fool of yourself that you know you are on to something.

"There are no right sides." I ration her one withering look. "Nothing changes. People talk about slavery like it's over, like it's a thing of the past, but there's no real difference between now and then. Except these days we keep our slaves out of sight and out of mind. They're in Africa or Asia, working for ten cents an hour. Instead of getting lashed by an overseer they're getting their hands chopped off by heavy-duty machinery. Is that so much better? People say plantation owners didn't see all the sin and corruption around them, but it's the same today. We gaze right through the horror our luxury is built on. That's what takes up ninety-nine percent of our mental energy, pretending slavery doesn't exist, pretending we're better than our bloodthirsty ancestors. But we're not." *In conclusion*, I add silently, pedantically, ". . . ain't nothing wrong with being a Confederate soldier."

There is a moment of silence. Then some old coot with a cane bangs it on the floor and says to no one in particular:

"Hot damn! She should run for public office!"

"Kara," Martin decides, "I believe you just talked yourself into the forces of General John S. Marmaduke's First Arkansas Battalion."

A few people applaud as I sit back down.

"My," Ilene observes, "you certainly have become accomplished at speaking."

"—don't like blue," I mutter, blushing. "It makes me look fat."

"Well, you got your wish. Speaking of which, I'm so glad you came by the house the other day."

"Did I? Oh yes."

"I could tell you brightened up Christy's mood. She could use the company. Being a new mother can be very isolating. You two should get out together. Go for a drive. I could take Shelby."

"Maybe," I shrug.

"What about some time next week? I've got nothing planned."

It is strange. A minute ago I was on my feet, lecturing my fellow townsfolk as I never would have dreamed of doing before, and now here I am sinking lower and lower in my seat, spinelessly agreeing to whatever this overbearing woman suggests, like I am fourteen again.

"I know you and Christy have a special relationship."

I breathe in the smell. It is money, all right. Money and power.

"Just don't wear blue," she adds roguishly.

I suppose I should have been shocked or nauseated, but I was not. Credit Saul. He made his wishes known in such a casual way, he was so certain of himself, that I never had to think. There was no question of refusal. It was part of the program, what we did on the Persian carpet, an extension of his role as mentor. And yes, I was flattered. He is still quite respected in the field, although many people assume he is dead. Some of those books whose spines I lingered over were his. I believed I was having (I know this sounds crazy) not just him, but his work, taking it in on a sub- or supra-intellectual level. Did I feel? That is what you might call a gray area. I felt his feeling, and was moved, excited by it. Maybe even proud. But, to be honest, it was just like sticking a finger in your ear . . . which you are not supposed to do, but which everyone does. Maybe that is the key. I felt like everybody else, for a change. He collected carved elephants, with their trunks raised. He told me it was a sign of good fortune. Sometimes I gazed up at the sexless undersides of optimistic elephants and thought, Here I am, at long last. At the center of things. What all the fuss is about.

An abortion costs four hundred seventy-nine dollars and eighty-eight cents. After brief consideration, I called someone for help. It was not, strictly speaking, the right thing to do, but ethics and morals were luxuries I could ill afford. Besides, I argued, by confiding in this person, I am giving her pleasure. So what if I have my own agenda? Whose actions are not ruled by self-interest?

"I decided cake is better," Miss Pitts explains, "because ice cream melts."

"—gives a whole new meaning to the expression 'crumb-bums,'" I risk, as we survey the attendees of my social, their laps and legs pretty much coated in the stuff.

"Oh, you are wicked."

You have no idea, I reflect.

"Kara has come all the way from New York City," she repeats, pitching her voice as if we are on an adjacent rooftop from these glazed and dazed octogenarians.

It is an unfair comparison, but out the window I can see several hundred hogs crowding around a trough at feeding time. They seem infinitely more alive. Even their grunts and whistles are more packed with meaning than the wan, semi-coherent responses we manage to coax forth from our crowd.

"I heard you had a tornado last summer."

"Goddamned agitators," one of them answers unexpectedly.

"It does whip things up."

The trick is to turn whatever they say into a conversation, despite the unpromising material. That is what I remember from my time here.

"You see him?"

Another has been clutching a wallet-size photo. It is almost mashed into a ball from constant display. I pretend to look.

"He's dead!" she says triumphantly.

"In the tornado?"

Corinne, the girl from under the bleachers, gives me a nudge.

"Why are her shoelaces untied?" someone demands.

"It's not a shoe." Corinne sticks her foot out, models it this way and that. "It's a sandal."

"It's a *scandal*," Miss Pitts corrects, and then giggles so hard she has to cover her mouth.

The surprise, for me, is discovering that Corinne occupies the exact same position I did at her age. She is the high school helper, though dressed more like a Goth mortician, and still sporting those deconstructed open-toed boots.

"I've got one last corner piece." I try tempting Mr. Robbins, the sole man who has deigned to join us. "Extra frosting. You want it, Mr. R?"

"Be careful," she murmurs, staring significantly at his crotch.

"Oh, I know all about that."

"Yeah, but I'm the one who has to clean him up."

"I do not have a family," Miss Pitts announces, tremblingly raising a plastic cup of Coca-Cola, "but when I take part in a gathering like this, I say to myself, Justine, you have *many families*."

Corinne and I smile gamely and, casting around, manage to find two plastic cups of our own, though hers, I notice, is filled with jelly beans. The others stare as if we, not they, are the demented.

"Do your nails grow like that?" a bent-over crone frowns, leaning forward to get a better view.

They are painted black and white. Not just by the toe. Each nail has several streaks.

"I play piano," Corinne explains. "This here's the middle three octaves."

"She's a shepherd!" Mr. Robbins bellows.

"Now, John."

Miss Pitts seems unusually upset by this.

"It's OK," I say. "He told me that before."

"Nevertheless, I do not want him disrupting our moment."

She gets up and—for her, a firm gesture—yanks him back without asking permission, before wheeling him off.

"Shepherd wouldn't be a bad job." Corinne picks through her jelly beans. "You get to sleep outside."

"I had you pegged more for a career in fashion," I say politely. "Are you doing this as part of a college plan?"

"No. I just wanted to get away from home."

"Really? You must have quite a situation."

"Got a piano," she shrugs, as if to say it is not so bad, and then ripples her toes, practicing scales.

"There!" Miss Pitts smiles, having returned from depositing Mr. Robbins. She contentedly surveys the remaining gridlock of wheelchairs. Most of the occupants are now snoozing off into sugar-induced comas. "I think that was a real treat for all involved."

"She shouldn't even be here," the one with the photo complains.

"I'm just waiting out the storm," I assure her.

"Storm?"

"The twister. Remember? Last summer? Tell me about it."

"Oh my, we had a time."

It is really not so different from a regular conversation, just that the inconsistency, the fundamental meaninglessness and circularity, is more starkly revealed. We are all bumbling along with our own trains of thought, only rarely and randomly intersecting.

"Corinne, would you mind cleaning up? I believe Kara and I have some business to attend to."

Miss Pitts goes off to her office. I apologize for not helping more, but Corinne is one of those phlegmatic types who does not seem to care.

"I'll make it up to you."

"It's OK," she says.

"You know, I once did this job."

"Yeah?"

"It's a good stepping-stone. Or can be."

She barely responds. I realize I am not as shining a role model as I once thought myself to be.

"She seems nice."

"She is," Miss Pitts sighs. "But, if I may speak frankly, she is not you."

"Seems pretty much like me. At her age, I mean."

"She doesn't have your sensibility."

What the hell's that supposed to mean? I feel like retorting. What do you think you know about me? About my "sensibility?" Just hand over the money. I am, all of a sudden, tortured with rage. I am supposed to be on a mission, looking for blood relatives, curing myself, single-handed, of a mortal disease. Instead I have been sidetracked by this sordid pregnancy business.

"I must apologize for Mr. Robbins. He is becoming a menace."

"I don't mind him."

"You don't mind anybody. You can afford not to mind people, what with your gifts."

My gifts? My sensibility? What is she talking about? I am the lowest of low, sitting here opposite her piled-high desk, using her for my own ends. I am as bad as anyone, if not worse.

She stares straight at me, deep into my nonexistent soul.

"I very much appreciate what you're doing," I blush.

"I never had a daughter."

"Well, a lot of things would have to happen first," I laugh nervously, "before you could even get around to considering that."

"But if I did have one, I would want her to be just like you."

"Really? I wouldn't. If I had a daughter, I'd want her to be . . ."

My mind trails off, lost in a swamp of improbability.

"You'd want her to be what?"

"I don't know. Less of a pain in the ass."

"I was that type of child," she says. "A very obedient girl."

. . . to which I can offer nothing, just a look around the room, with its ever-accumulating forms and ever-more-antiquated equipment. The setting, all by itself, provides a damningly silent commentary. She is still that obedient child.

"It's in twenties." She hands me an envelope. "I hope that's all right."

"Don't you want to know what it's for?"

"No."

"I'll pay you back."

"I'm sure you will. But you take your time about it."

"I was afraid you'd be . . ." I look down and wonder if I am really addressing myself, "disappointed."

"On the contrary."

I wait for more, but that seems to be all she has to say, so I get up. Then she starts talking, not to me though. Not directly. It is as if I have inadvertently pressed a button, releasing a steady stream of words.

"I remember one time, my mother took me to an Easter egg hunt. There was a field. I have no idea where. And candy had been laid, chocolate eggs and bunnies, all over. It just dotted the landscape, like it was the natural crop that grew. We all stood at the edge with these baskets we'd been given, and then, at a certain moment, everyone rushed forward. Except me. I don't know why. I remember my mother pushing me, pointing at the treats, but I couldn't move. All I could do was clutch my basket and watch. She was getting more and more angry. Finally, she started grabbing stuff herself. She was down there with the little kids, furious at me. I could sense that."

"What were you looking for?"

"I have no idea." She continues to stare where I was, even though by now I am standing at the door. "I still don't."

Corinne pokes her head in.

"Mr. Robbins wet himself."

"You put that son of a bitch in diapers."

"He don't like it when—"

"Tell him if he makes a fuss I'm going to come out and cram those urine-soaked drawers down his throat myself."

Corinne nods like she is actually memorizing the message, then withdraws.

"Cool nail job," I say, trying to redirect her rather unnerving attention from the empty chair.

"She's not you."

"Well, I don't think *I'm* me, anymore. To be honest."

"You will be. Once you get out of here."

"Get out of here? You mean get out of Witch's Falls? I thought you wanted me to stay."

She looks up and smiles.

"We had our social," she says. "Wasn't it grand?"

CHAPTER EIGHT

"Drank a cup of coffee. Right there at Kreski's."

"What's so unusual about that?"

"Gladys Dawes? She hasn't had spirits or a stimulating beverage of any kind for as long as people here can remember."

"Why? Is she a Jehovah's Witness?"

"No. She says she just doesn't like the taste."

"Of coffee?"

"Of anything. Anything that might affect her natural metabolism. It's more of a health issue. Though she is, of course, a Baptist."

"Of course," I nod knowingly.

It is terrible timing. I arrived just before the end, hoping to be the last, so no one would see me and so the rent-a-priest they have coming in for the day would let me off easy, wanting to get going himself. But instead I am stuck with Mrs. Tom Green, wife of Major Tom Green (Ret.), both of whom have known me since I was a little girl. She is in her seventies now, wearing a faded linen jacket the same color as her skin, what you might call blown chrysanthemum.

"It's good to see you, Kara."

"Where's the Major?"

"He lost his faith," she announces briskly.

"Oh no."

"Same as his daddy. I suppose it's something all the Greens do. Or go through, I should say, since he did receive the consolations of the church on his deathbed. The Major's father, that is."

"Well, thank heaven for that."

"Yes."

"Still, it must be upsetting, not to have him come here with you anymore."

"I have to believe for both of us now."

"So it's strengthened your own certainty."

"You might say."

Finally, the person ahead of us, who has been confessing to a series of axe murders, judging by the time he took, scurries up the aisle.

"You tell your mother hello," Mrs. Green says, rising, and with a stiff stateliness enters the box.

I believe in keeping my word. I do not know why, though. Does it not imply that the rest of the time we are merely mouthing half truths, if not retailing outright lies? Then, in a shocking departure, we agree to do what we say? Still, since I seem to have sullied Mrs. Dawes's previously spotless reputation to the extent that the community now believes she is slavishly addicted to caffeine, the least I can do is fulfill my promise to consult a man of the cloth. The trick is to tell one who cannot see me, does not know who I am, and is powerless to do anything more serious than threaten eternal damnation. I do not believe in God, but I see no logical objection to believing in other people's belief. Mrs. Green, say, redoubling her efforts, trying to drag her reluctant husband through the pearly gates. That, to me, is admirable. And touching.

Nevertheless, I have come on a Wednesday, when Mother shows houses in the evening and then stays late doing accounts back at the office. I do not want her to think I have any renewed interest in this place. Organized religion never made a very deep impression on me, pro or con. I am not a joiner.

Mrs. Green takes twenty seconds, emerging as she would from a toilet stall and—in a state of grace—sweeps on out of the church. The heavy front door echoes. It occurs to me that I should have prepared some arguments or at least a few one-liners, as I would before leading an undergraduate discussion group, but I am so tired.

"Forgive me, Father, it has been, oh Lord, quite some time since my last confusion. *Confession*," I correct, and then begin to laugh.

"How long?"

It is a young man's voice, which sobers me a little, not that of the faceless stick who came around last time. In my day, the priest was inevitably some doddering old charlatan performing Mass with all the panache of a drunk magician. Once, the diocese promised to send a more alert representative, but he turned out to be from black Africa. That nearly caused a riot. I forget what his real name was. Everyone called him Father Oingo-Boingo. He did not last long. Complaints were made. I would love to hear his side of the story. What he thought of us.

"Going on seven years, two months," I calculate.

"That certainly is a long time. How do you know so precisely?"

"I came with my mother. I was just about to go off to college."

"And when you left home you stopped attending?"

His voice has that Irishness to it. A lilt. He sounds almost my age, if such a thing is possible.

"I found the church wanting."

"Wanting in what?"

"Intellectual rigor."

"I see."

This is not going along the lines I had envisioned. I try wrenching the process back on course.

115

"The thing is: I promised someone I would come and talk to you about a problem I was having. But I have to warn you in advance that nothing you say is going to change my mind. Because really it's none of your business. I'm just discharging an obligation."

"Is there a sin somewhere in this rigmarole?" he asks, with a hint of impatience.

"Oh yes. A big one. Mortal, I assume."

"And what might that be?"

"Excuse me, but where are you from? If you don't mind my asking. Originally, I mean?"

"Surely that's not going to help us deal with the parlous state of your soul, my child."

"The what?"

"I said—"

"Parlous? Did you say *parlous?*"

"It means precarious. I was simply trying to indicate that you seem to be in danger, and that is what we should be focusing on, not where I—"

"Yes, I know what *parlous* means. I'm just really impressed that you said it out loud. I've never heard that word used in conversation before."

"This is hardly a conversation."

"Well, it's not a modern dance recital."

"What?"

"I mean of course it's a conversation. Are you from Ireland? Because that's what it sounds like."

There is a pause. I am kneeling, of course.

"Yes. I am from Galway. A town on the western coast of Ireland."

"I thought so!"

Oh god, Kara, a voice inside me sneers, why don't you just hike up your skirt and flash a bit of thigh, the way you did to that guy on the telephone six thousand miles away in Bangalore?

116

For one thing, I am not wearing a skirt, I point out silently. And as for that other man, he managed to totally reinstall my operating system at no charge!

Is that what you're hoping for here?

No, but—

"...something about a mortal sin?" he prompts.

"Yes, I'm sorry. I am pregnant by a seventy-five-year-old philosopher of the analytic school, and tomorrow I am going to get an abortion."

He coughs. At least I think it is a cough.

"Where, if you don't mind my asking, in this godforsaken wilderness does one find a seventy-five-year-old philosopher of . . . the analytic school, you say?"

"Oh, that didn't happen here. I'm just down on a visit. Reconnecting with family and friends. Unwinding."

"How pleasant."

"So like I said, I promised this woman I would talk to someone, that I would consult a member of the clergy, and that's you. You are a priest, aren't you?"

"Of course I'm a priest! What the hell do you think I'm doing here?"

"Sorry."

"No, I'm sorry. I shouldn't have said that."

"It's just that you sound so young. Is this your first . . . ?"

"Yes," he answers patiently, "This is my first parish. I recently completed a program that offered educational subsidies in return for my serving abroad for several years. Now, the church teaches that abortion is, indeed, a terrible sin. Have you considered adoption?"

"Look, I have an appointment for ten o'clock tomorrow morning. It's a done deal."

"Then why are you here?"

"I told you, I promised someone."

"You seem too intelligent a person not to see through that flimsy pretext. Clearly you are having doubts about what you are about to do. There is no reason why you can't take this pregnancy to term then give the child to a loving family."

"I also have cancer. So if I have this baby it will vastly increase my chances of dying prematurely."

"Oh."

I feel bad for the guy. This is not a set of circumstances they ran by him in whatever bargain basement seminary he attended. And then to be sent here! I am sure he imagined saving souls in the Third World, not listening to Mrs. Tom Green harbor lustful thoughts concerning the postman.

"How do you like the food?" I ask.

"You have cancer," he repeats.

"It must be different than where you come from."

"Christ, it's awful," he groans. "Do you know what I was served the other day? Snicker Salad. It's chopped-up apples and Snicker bar."

"Snickers, actually. Even one is plural. I don't know why. You should be flattered. That's considered something of a delicacy."

"It was all I could do not to wretch in my hostess's face."

"You know what I say in that situation? 'It's too rich for me.'"

"Oh, that's a good one. I must remember that. 'It's too rich for me.' You've consulted your doctor?"

"Yes."

"What a dreadful dilemma."

"Not really. I mean, it sucks, but I've been kind of happy since I got here. Maybe in a melancholy way, but so much better than when I was growing up. I was really miserable, then."

"One is never more tormented than in one's teens."

"I guess not."

"The doctrine on the subject is pretty clear. I feel duty bound to warn that you are at risk, theologically speaking, no matter what you do."

"That's hardly news."

"Do you still pray?"

"No. I mean not in a formalized, conventional way. I ask for things. A seat on the subway. Not . . . too much pain."

"That is not prayer. That is a child's grabbing. Your penance is—"

"Penance? I haven't done anything wrong."

"—your penance," he insists, "is to pray. Sincerely and earnestly."

"Oh, I can't do that. I can't pray for my soul or divine guidance or any of that mumbo jumbo."

"I am not asking you to. I am asking you to pray for me, for my salvation. And I, in turn, will pray for you. For your health and well-being. For your being graced with the wisdom to make the right decision and for your complete recovery."

"Deal," I shrug. "If you don't mind my saying so, that's a sucker's bet. Your prayers have got to be more powerful than mine. I expect any tumors I have left to start shriveling up right away."

"Stranger things have happened."

"So where are you off to next? Have you tried the new Baconator Menu at Denny's?"

But, like with a shrink, our time is up. He intones the formula:

"Give thanks to the Lord, for He is good."

. . . to which I automatically respond:

"His mercy endures forever."

I check his name plate on the way out. Rev. Denis Donovan.

Maybe he's not as much of a rube as I took him for, I decide, walking through town. Maybe he'll make pope.

The light is on in Mother's office. Lifted by a wave of daughterly love, I decide to drop in on her. I cross the street but, as I do, the light goes off. She must be closing up. I wait for her to come out.

119

Why is one "never more tormented than in one's teens"? I continue the dialogue.

Because one is never closer to a sense of mystical awareness than at that age. And it is devastating, the gap such an awareness illuminates. Though lately . . .

She does not emerge. The office is now dark. I try the door. It is locked. The cardboard clock, with its moveable hands, says BACK AT 9:00 A.M. I knock.

"Ma?" I ask, into the silence.

Frowning, I try the door again. There is definitely someone in there. Or was. A burglar?

Main Street is nothing more than a strip of stores separated every few hundred feet by alleyways. In back are parking spaces for merchants and miniature dumpsters, unflattering counterparts to the carefully maintained displays and striped awnings out front. I know the area well. We used to play here as kids. I pass through the blasting exhaust of Osage Pizza and peer between the rusting bars that block most of the window to her tiny private office. Sounds are coming from inside. There is a fluttering curtain. I manage to reach in and grab a handful, thrusting it aside. On the daybed, in the far corner, my mother is being raped.

"Ma!" I scream.

Actually, she is on top, I note, as my eyes adjust. There is some hideous bearish man underneath her, all matted hair, struggling to disengage himself. Neither of them is completely undressed. It is like a scene from a science-fiction film. She has a panicked expression. Something has taken over her brain.

"Kara?"

She squints in my direction. I let go of the curtain, but the damage is done. What am I going to do? I cannot just run. I back away until I am engulfed in the grease fumes being vented by the pizzeria's industrial fan. They feel strangely cleansing after what I just saw.

120

But did I really see anything? I argue hopefully. Is it possible I am about to wake up? Preferably in Honolulu?

The heavy bolt of the service door shoots back. Mother appears, still in sartorial disarray. Her blouse is not tucked into her skirt. It gives her a kind of girls-boarding-school look.

"Kara?" she calls again, not seeing me.

I step forward into the light.

"Didn't know what to do," I mumble. "I thought you were being attacked."

"You better come inside."

"Oh, that's OK. You go back to whatever it was you were— I mean, we're all adults here."

"Inside. Now," she orders, retrieving her parental mojo, and turns, knowing I will follow.

The room is too small for three, especially when one is the size of a house. I refer to the man, who stands self-consciously, as if at a cocktail party. He is wearing recently pulled-up sweatpants and has covered his hairy chest with a shirt that boasts some kind of insignia. I try not to meet his eyes. Or any other part of his gargantuan frame.

"Kara, this is Mr. John Kiperstein. John, this is my daughter Kara . . ."

"Holy crap, you are dating a Jew!" I exclaim, remembering the yarmulke incident.

". . . whom you've heard so much about."

"Pleased to meet you."

He has a booming voice. And about a size twenty-five hand. After we shake, I unthinkingly wipe mine against my jeans.

"Your mother's so proud of you," he smiles.

"Wait a minute." I identify the logo on his shirt. An eagle. "You're that guy. Coach Kip!"

"I am, indeed."

121

"That's what we have to talk to you about," Mother says, with a pained look, sitting at her desk. "Why don't you sit?"

She motions to the daybed.

"You've got to be kidding. I'm not sitting there."

"John and I have been seeing each other for quite some time now."

He moves over and puts his hands on her shoulders, an old-fashioned gesture. What you see on a family Christmas card.

"However, it's not a relationship we feel is ready for public notice, quite yet."

"Why? Is he married?"

"I am, in a sense."

"John is in the process of getting a divorce," Mother explains. "And there is some disagreement about what is best for the child."

"Custardy battle," he frowns. "My lawyer tells me it's better if I don't appear to be involved, for the present."

"She's not here," Mother adds hastily. "She's in Chicago. Both are. John's soon-to-be ex-wife and his daughter."

"Custardy battles can often hinge on perception."

I feel I should ream out my ears. Everything he says sounds slightly off. "Custardy battle" makes me see a grown man and wo-man going at it with spoonfuls of My-T-Fine Chocolate Pudding.

"So you meet at night, in the office? That's the only time you can be together?"

"No. In the past, John came to the house."

"Oh. But now that I'm back . . . ?"

"We didn't want to upset you."

"Does Gerald know?"

"Gerald and I have an understanding."

"He's a fine young man," Coach Kip offers.

I am irrationally and profoundly *furious*. Mother never dated, all through our growing up. At least not that she allowed us to see.

I recall her fending men off, their unwanted advances, that fake solicitude they would show her, and us; how they squatted down to make eye contact, asked dumb questions, pinched our cheeks. "How would you like to throw a football around, little feller?" "She's going to be a real heartbreaker, someday." And she being so firmly polite while, at the same time, so obviously dismissive. Obvious to me, but not always to them. Some would come around again and again. She would sigh as a doomed suitor too dense to take the hint made his way across the parking lot. "Let me help you with those groceries, Jeannie." "We're doing fine, thanks." But he would take them anyway, with a comical display of strength. I could see how their muscles went right on up into their heads, how their brains were nothing more than a continuation of clueless bone and gristle. Or so it seemed to a child, holding her mother's hand while another paunchy would-be Romeo loaded our trunk.

Now it turns out she has not been keeping herself pure at all! And maybe never had, that whole time. By the light of one blinding revelation I have to re-see my entire past, which I cannot do, of course, not all at once, mainly because the man in question is standing two feet away from me and my jaw is still sticking out like the drawer of a cash register.

"We felt that because of your condition," she begins, "it was better to be discreet."

Coach Kip clears his throat.

"I'm very much in love with your mother."

I can see him now: an awkward blowhard, with genuine feelings, no doubt, and a smidgeon of small-town charisma, decent "husband material," as the ladies around here would say.

"Once I'm free to do so, I intend to ask for her hand."

. . . which he then, just to cement his claim to be the most literal-minded man alive, proceeds to do, takes her hand, illustrating what he has just said in case I am too dense to get it via language. And she just sits there, simpering, letting him tenderize it like a veal cutlet.

"Congratulations."

"The point is," she pulls away from him, all business, suddenly, "nobody can know about this."

"Right," I nod. "The custardy battle."

"Custardy," he corrects.

So he can hear it, but can't say it. He is mentally retarded. My future stepfather belongs in a Home. Which, by train of natural association, leads me to ask:

"Wait a minute. Where are you going to live?"

"John and I both think that the best solution is to make a fresh start. I've had my eye on several properties. Of course we're not in a position to make a bid on anything yet, but—"

"You're going to sell our house?"

"My house," she says gently. "I was only keeping it until you and Gerald were old enough. Now that Gerald's in business for himself, I'm sure he wants to spread his wings a bit, as do I."

"There will always be a room for you, Kara," Coach assures me, "wherever we end up. I can call you Kara, can't I?"

"What else would you call me?"

The look Mother has is soft and contented. Nothing you can say is going to change this, it seems to convey. Our family, as you know it, is *gone*.

And why not? I ask myself on the way home. She has done her duty by us, plus so much more. Why should she not have a little fun? A second chapter? A new beginning? It just makes me feel so superfluous, is all.

"Sorry you had to find out that way," she says.

"How were you going to tell me? Send an invitation to your wedding?"

"About that, are you by any chance interested in being my maid of honor?"

"Oh please."

"It would be a good way for you to get to know your stepsister."

"I have no interest in getting to know anyone."

"She's fifteen. He wants her for summers and vacations, which is right, of course. But she is a handful."

"Worse than me?"

"You were no trouble at all. Never have been. You're my pride and joy."

I am facing away from her. There is a wadded-up sweater prodding the small of my back. I dig it up and throw it behind me. The nest, I realize, is largely of my own devising.

"He's a good man, Kara."

"I can see that. But good enough for you to put up with being the Other Woman? Sneaking out? Being in the wrong? That couldn't have been fun."

"No. It hasn't been," she admits.

"And don't football coaches move around a lot? If they're successful?"

"That is something I am willing to do."

"You mean give up your business and everything? He must be the real deal."

"You have no idea."

"Well, that's great, Ma." I turn to her. "I wish you all the happiness in the world."

"He fills me up."

"That's nice," I frown, sensing another confidence I do not want to be made privy to.

"The first time, when I saw it, I actually wondered, *Can I contain this?* I mean in the military sense."

"That's great, Ma," I repeat blankly. "I wish you all the happiness in the world."

"It does make me curious—and I hope you won't mind my asking—but I don't understand how someone with your proclivities can achieve true satisfaction."

"Proclivities? What proclivities?"

"I mean, it must be like . . ." She frowns. ". . . being a vegetarian is how I picture it."

"I can walk from here. If you'll just slow down a bit. Otherwise I'm going to have to jump from the speeding vehicle."

"Oh, don't be so prudish, Kara. You're twenty-three years old. Can't we have an adult conversation?"

"I can. But it sounds to me like he's drilled you back to some Stone Age–cheerleader state."

"I feel alive. That's all."

"What did you feel the whole time we were growing up? Were you doing stuff like this back then? Getting it on in a car with someone's husband while you were supposed to be at a PTA meeting?"

"Of course not!"

"'Cause I remember there were guys—"

"I wouldn't give those pasty-faced excuses for men the time of day, when you two were young."

"So you just had none of those feelings at all for twenty years?"

"That was a very difficult portion of my life," she answers carefully. "Beautiful, but difficult."

"And it's over now?"

"Yes, it is. For you too. That's what I'm trying to tell you. Trying to show you."

"Oh, so this is all for my benefit."

"No, but it wouldn't hurt for you to realize."

"Realize what?"

We pull into the driveway.

"Oh," I remember. "I ran into Mrs. Tom Green. She says hello. Did you know that the Major no longer goes to church? He lost his faith."

"Getting caught playing strip poker with a bunch of casino hostesses in Biloxi will do that to you."

The house is dark. Gerald is out, of course. It galls me that he knew and I did not, galls me even more that he did not tell.

"Realize what?" I ask again at the base of the stairs. "What am I supposed to be learning from all this?"

"Oh, I don't know." She looks weary. "Just that your pursuit of all these accomplishments, admirable as it may be, is also a running away from things. Look at me. I spent almost my entire youth denying a whole side of my existence so I could concentrate on raising you children and making something of myself. And I'm proud of that, don't get me wrong, but there comes a time when you have to turn around and deal with whatever it was that set you on that path in the first place."

"But I'm still just starting out."

"That's the point. I don't want you to put it off as long as I did. Because, I don't know if you've noticed this in my case, but it makes you kind of crazy. I mean just now, in the car, talking about John, I heard words coming out of my mouth that I could hardly credit."

"I guess you left your sexuality too long on the back burner."

"Try the deep freeze. It's not a mistake I'd like to see you repeat."

We hug. She waits, in case I experience another power failure on the steps. I hesitate, then ask:

"Will I have to wear a dress?"

"We're talking at least a year in the future."

"The dress could be a deal-breaker."

"I've always been partial to fuchsia."

I make a face.

"I would also expect a shower," she warns.

Upstairs, I can barely pull off my clothes. They stink of pizza and incense. I get into bed and then, so a nagging sense of neglected duty will not keep me awake, get out and kneel, with my head against the mattress.

"Denis Donovan," I remember, miraculously, considering what has happened since. "Give him everything he wants. Peace. Happiness. The courage to face Snickers Salad and all the other horrors of his calling."

True prayer, of course, has to be addressed to Someone. I take the opportunity to reintroduce myself.

"Thank you, Lord. Amen."

Back under the sheets, I snuggle down, awash in that nostalgia of well-being from childhood.

"Tomorrow: Commit Mortal Sin," I murmur, going over my mental to do list, then sleep.

CHAPTER NINE

"I can't believe you're wearing heels."

"Well, I didn't know how to dress." Christy, driving, looks over. "You look like a delegate to the National Janitors Convention."

"I'm having a surgical procedure. You don't go fancy for that."

"I would. I would want to be the most sensational-looking baby-killer in the room. That would be my philosophy. God, it's good to be on the road."

It is. I just wish I could forget the reason we are speeding down Route 167 in her luxury sedan. The child seat in back is empty. We are truly free.

"What did you tell Martin?"

"I didn't tell him nothing. Girls' day out. He doesn't care."

"What about Ilene?"

"She acted like it was her idea."

"I guess it was." I think back to her badgering me at the pageant meeting. "Although she doesn't know the cause."

"I don't consider that the cause. I consider that a chore we have to get out of the way before having some fun. I can't tell you how confined I have felt over the past year."

"By the baby?"

"The baby's just an outgrowth. A natural result of the boredom. It's like he's a symptom."

"Of what disease?"

"Nothing. Being alone in that house. Being alone together."

"But I thought you said it was good between you two."

"It is. I *love* Martin."

"You make that sound like a bad thing."

"It's complicated."

She has a better fashion sense than I remember from high school. Of course she had no money, then. Now, she is wearing very sleek capri pants, designer sunglasses, and a gauzy kerchief knotted under her chin.

"You ever think about running away?"

"Only every day, around sunset. That's when I make myself a special cocktail."

"Long Island Iced Tea?"

"...'cause it reminds me of you. Ooo, look!"

A scruffy teenaged boy is standing by the side of the road, with a sign reading DALLAS.

"No," I plead.

But it is too late. She is already slowing down. He breaks into a trot.

"How you-all doing?"

She pushes up her sunglasses and turns her charm on him like a very wide, very bright light, the kind they point at a prisoner when he tries to escape. I know the feeling, having been caught in its glare myself. But that does not make me any more sympathetic to his intruding upon our moment, or what threatened to become our moment, which is, of course, why she stopped in the first place.

...'cause it reminds me of you.

Yet I have rarely thought of Christy since leaving Witch's Falls. Not like that. Not in a longing, wistful way. Is it possible—I gingerly entertain the notion, as if it might be radioactive—that I could give her something she genuinely needs?

He is Jeremy and going to visit a sister who lives in "the Metroplex area." He keeps calling it that. He has memorized the phrase.

What would it be like, I lazily consider while she chats him up, to cut young Jeremy here into little pieces and bury them along the side of the road?

"And exactly what do you study?" she asks, pretending to be a lecherous housewife.

"Well ma'am, I'm going to Ozarka Community College in the fall, so I don't rightly know yet."

"Physical education?" she suggests, nudging me.

I turn to confirm that, yes, he has that casually alive body boys briefly possess before they subside into blubber. I am not immune. I am, after all, a product of the culture, albeit an unwilling one. But male sexuality is so fundamentally boring as to put me to sleep, or force me to work rather. The golden-haired chest, hinted at under worn cotton, incites in me an obscene itch to reread the Tractatus. "Whereof one cannot speak, thereof one must be silent." And all that implies. A world beyond the mundane.

"And how about you ladies?"

He is a well-mannered young man. It is a pity that, enacting an ancient fertility rite, we are going to plant his sexual parts at the base of our temple and sprinkle his blood over the fields.

"What are you up to today?"

"We are open to offers," Christy chirps. "My friend here has to see her doctor, but that shouldn't take too long. After, the only item on our agenda is F-U-N."

"In Little Rock?"

"That's right."

"What does your sister do?" I ask.

"She's married."

I wait for more, but it is not forthcoming.

"... has two children," he finally adds. "Boys."

"Isn't that nice," Christy sighs.

He notices the car seat.

"I see you have one."

"Had," she corrects. "Poor thing."

There is a silence. He edges away from it, closer to the window.

"I'm sorry to hear that."

"That's all right. I keep it, the seat, as a kind of reminder. It's like— What were you telling me about, Kara, that they used to do in medieval times?"

"I don't know what you mean."

"Sure you do. You told me once, when we were in high school— we've known each other forever—that people used to keep a skull, or a skeleton, at parties, just to remind them . . . ?"

"Oh, memento mori. A reminder of death. I can't believe you remember my telling you that."

I am almost embarrassingly excited. I press my knees together. Where do these feelings come from? And why? Because she held close to her some factoid that interested me when I was sixteen? Because she responded, even if at a remove, to something I exulted in discovering? Did my enthusiasm make such an impression? A crazy life pops up before my mind's eye. The two of us together in Brooklyn, me resuming my studies and she . . . what? Listening at the end of the day as I talk about my work, as I think out loud? Does such a nerdy vision even qualify as a fantasy?

"My poor little girl." Christy produces a sob. I notice though she has changed the gender, so as not to jinx Shelby. "Taken from me too soon."

"Well, that's awful," he stammers.

"It's all right," I smile. "The court found her not responsible."

"They did?"

"... for her actions."

"... for my *inactions*. I allowed her to drown, you see."

"Oh Lord."

"It's a vision I'll take with me to my dying day."

"Well, that's why you should get rid of the car seat," I argue.

"I can't. It's always there. Every time I look back."

"That's because it really *is* there."

"How old are your little nephews, Jeremy?"

"Who?" He is having trouble keeping up. "Oh. They're just babies. One's not even a year. The other's maybe two or three?"

"I'd love to meet them. Do they look like you?"

"I don't know. They don't look like much of anything, yet."

"Still unformed," she sighs. "They're so cute at that age. I'll bet they look just like you."

"The Metroplex is Satan's parlor," I warn. "Lots of dangerous people there. You take care of yourself. Someone stops their car and offers you a ride like we did, don't just get in without looking first. Without evaluating the situation. Understand?"

"Yes, ma'am," he swears.

"Evil walks abroad."

He nods.

"... in the Metroplex."

We let him off outside the city limits. It will be easier for him to get a ride that way. He seems pretty eager, slamming the door like he just survived a close call.

"Ozarka College," she sniffs. "I applied there."

"There's not a single thing they could have taught you."

"Damn right. Now where is this clinic?"

"Just off South Shackleford."

"That's not near anything."

133

"Probably by design."

"Yeah, but I thought I could scope out the neighborhood while you were inside. Maybe find us a place to go shopping, after."

"I don't think I'm going to be in any sort of condition."

"You're going to be fine. I wish you'd stop brooding. You know the expression PACE? Bet they didn't teach you that in graduate school."

"PACE?"

"Positive Attitude Changes Everything. Here it is. Now let's go and get you all fixed up."

"It's not a beauty salon."

As we walk from the car to the front door, a man emerges out of nowhere. He is brandishing a huge pickle jar.

"Miss!" he calls. "Miss, wait!"

He gets between us and the entrance, thrusting what I now see is a sloshing embryo about an inch from my nose.

"Before you go in there, Miss, I think you ought to know—"

The rest of his speech is one long keening whine as Christy drives the point of her stiletto heel through the top of his shoe, penetrating whatever reptilian claw he possesses down there.

"See? I told you it's important to dress properly for these occasions," she says, shielding me from his screams, escorting me on in.

I put my hand to my face and find it is wet.

"Did he spit on me?"

"I just hope he doesn't vandalize my car."

"You can go, now. I'll be OK from here."

"Don't be ridiculous."

I give my name to a woman sitting behind bulletproof glass.

"And you are?" she asks Christy.

"I am the child's father."

We go to a room with magazines.

"Seriously," I say. "Get out of here. Go have some fun, like you were talking about."

"This is fun. This is exactly what I've been missing."

She stays until they take me. It will be a few hours, we are warned. "Go," I urge.

"You take extra-special care of that girl," she calls after us, as the nurse leads me off. "That there's the governor's daughter!"

I am careful, answering all the questions, to lie about my lymphoma. My hair has grown back just enough to make me look weird rather than "compromised," a status I have already been classified as on quite enough medical forms. There follows a gruesome act of state-sponsored terrorism where they try to make me feel like I have blood dripping from my fingernails just from taking charge of my own body. That, paradoxically, strengthens my resolve. You really would have to be nothing more than a brainless, spineless, baby-making machine to be spooked out of having an abortion by the screeds they are obliged to recite and the pictures they are legally required to show.

"How very Christian," I offer politely, after the last, and affix my name to the consent decree with all the fervor of a patriot signing the Declaration of Independence.

The second waiting room I go to is not as much fun as the first. There are teary-eyed teenage girls here, as well as shame-faced older women. I am not a union organizer, but it does seem like promising territory for some sort of agitation, all of us in our humiliating hospital gowns, being made to feel like dirt, while the other half of the equation, the other responsible party, is nowhere to be found, is represented, insofar as I can tell, only by that limping hate-filled zealot out in the parking lot.

"Abortion is murder!" I now realize he was screaming as Christy hustled me inside.

"Yes, and so is paying your taxes, over half of which goes to much more efficient, systematic killing on an unprecedented scale . . . of those who have actually managed to be born!"

People look at me. I realize I have been muttering under my breath and physically clamp my lips shut.

Then they call me in.

Regret. I hate regret. What exactly is the point? Done is done. You cannot change things. Regret is who you are, a record of your missteps, and what are missteps but the path you have chosen?

A jagged bolt of grief rips apart the night sky over my head. It is light and dark at the same time. I hear the doctor murmuring and the clink of cutlery. This is a failing restaurant. I am the sole meal being served.

Won't you stay? I ask, addressing both the It that will never be and the Me that is now irrevocably altered. Won't you stick around for just a little while longer?

We will, they answer in unison, as haunting half creatures, fairies and goblins, inhabitants of dreams and reveries.

I am sorry.

I try to see regret as an act, not some watered-down feeling.

Is this prayer? I wonder.

"Suction," a voice says.

They wheel me out. I feel great. Euphoric.

"It's the anesthesia," the nurse cautions. "It wears off."

In the recovery room, home to the least pregnant people on Earth, there is an office party atmosphere, with items (apple juice, saltines) no one has eaten since childhood.

"Well, I learned my lesson," a girl proclaims.

. . . one so obvious, apparently, that she feels no need to say what it is.

Another woman is crying continuously.

"I'm fine," she keeps saying, through tears. "I'm just fine."

I feel the wonderful sense of a wall reasserting itself. Breached, I was briefly subject to feeling. Now, flooded by relief and opiates, I feel the pendulum swing all the way back and achieve an almost cryogenic calm. Life is a board game again. I will roll the dice and proceed six squares. Doubles? I will roll again. If not, I will wait my turn, fingering my money and Get Out of Jail Free card. The squares do not permit any outrageous reinterpretation of the rules. Whatever emotions I experienced while they were doing it were removed along with everything else.

"Your friend is here."

I nod sagely. I have commanded her existence by determining it was time to go.

I know it is the drugs, their aftereffects. Confidence is just as manufactured a feeling as despair. But what it brings out is truly inside me. I just have to emphasize that part of me more. Witch's Falls has a tendency to encourage the opposite: laziness, lax reasoning, diminished expectations. People set goals so absurdly attainable they could just as easily be labeled inevitabilities. I was raised here, yes. By accident. My aim is, and always has been, to get out. In every sense. My mistake, before, was thinking it was only a question of geography. It is not.

"Temperature, extreme discomfort, heavy discharge . . ." the nurse runs through all the things that can go wrong.

This time, when I leave, I will take with me that which makes me whole, so I am no longer some stunted freak denying half her emotions, but a veritable Superwoman, crushing the world's opposition beneath my feet!

. . . in shoes I have yet to buy, I note, appalled, as they return my drab attire.

Christy is waiting just inside the door.

"I have a surprise for you," she grins.

"Me too," I say, deciding, *I am going to make you my wife.*

The car is pulled up front, with the engine running, so Pickle Dick, she explains, having named him in my absence, cannot intercept us. But someone is already sitting in the front seat. A stranger.

"I stowed the baby seat in the trunk. Thought you might need more room." Christy opens the rear door. "Maybe you want to lie down?"

"Hello, Kara."

I slide into the back, not really understanding. The stranger turns, and I see the dark glasses. It is Amy, the Mormon missionary. But that makes no sense. Am I hallucinating? The car takes off like a rocket. I grab at one of the handles.

"How was your extraction?" she asks.

"I told her about your dental problems." Christy hastily accelerates out of the parking lot. I hear yelling behind us. A crowd of protestors. "You OK?"

"Fine," I answer. "How did you—?"

"Only one Outreach Center in Little Rock." She turns to Amy. "Kara told me all about your dinner. She couldn't stop saying what an amazing speaker you were."

"I knew we had established a connection," Amy says solemnly. "How's your mouth?"

"Yes." Christy glances in the mirror to drive home the lie. "Your mouth. They finally pull that tooth?"

"I'm fine," I repeat.

"You don't sound different," Amy notes. "Did they give you Novocain?"

"It must have wore off."

"Good." Christy nods vigorously. "We don't want you drooling all over the upholstery back there."

I rather self-consciously sit up, remembering "temperature, extreme discomfort, heavy discharge," all of which I seem to be experiencing at once.

"There were no shops anywhere," Christy complains. "No boutiques, no dress stores, nothing. And I've been to that sorry excuse for a mall about seven hundred times already. Then I remembered you telling how you met this lovely young lady out in Booneville, of all places. So I punched up Mormon Outreach Center on the directions gizmo—"

"The church prefers to be known as LDS. It stands for Latter-Day Saints."

"—and here we are."

"I think I'm going to faint," I warn.

"I know just what you mean. I'm excited too. Now the question is, where should the three of us go?"

Little Rock is famous for having absolutely nothing to do or see. There is the Big Dam Bridge, "the largest pedestrian bridge in the world built specifically for that use," a curving, endless cement walkway. There is the Heifer Village, run by the Heifer Foundation, which attempts to solve the problem of world hunger by exporting cows. But in the end, it really is not much of a decision. We take her to the site of many school field trips, La Petite Roche Plaza, a strip of land on the Arkansas River boasting the actual "little rock" after which the city was so inauspiciously named.

"Feel," Christy orders, guiding Amy's hand over the rough surface and embedded bronze plaque. "That's what you call living history."

We get her set up on the grass and then go off to a nearby snack stand to bring back food.

"What the hell are you doing?" I complain.

"I thought you'd be happy. Didn't you tell me she was getting Gerald's genealogical records?"

"Yes, but she doesn't know he's my brother. And even if she did, I could hardly ask her to just run me off a copy."

"Kara, Kara, Kara," Christy sighs, putting her arm around me. "Don't you know how to succeed in life? People are like snails."

"Because they're slow? Or because they have hideous antennae?"

"Because you have to stick a little fork inside them and wiggle it all around to get the good stuff out."

"That is one truly nauseating image. And when did you ever eat snails?"

"On my honeymoon."

When we get back, Amy has laid several pamphlets on the ground.

"'The LDS and You,'" Christy reads. "Oh, here's one. 'Chastity.'"

"I'm required to put these out," she explains. "I'm on duty."

"It must be hard," I sympathize.

"It's God's work. But it can be a bit lonely."

"Well, that's why I thought you might want to see Kara again. Your boss seemed very understanding."

"You made it sound like she had questions about the church."

"I do," I manage to say. "But I'm sorry to hear that you're lonely. Don't you people usually travel in pairs?"

"We're missionaries, not swans."

"I know, but—"

"Yes, I do have a mission-year partner. But we don't get along. I think she finds my disability a burden."

"And you don't?"

"Of course not. It's how the Lord made me. It's part of His plan. If I was sighted, perhaps you wouldn't feel as free to talk to me the way you do. I sense you're a very guarded person."

I am, once again, intrigued by how her appearance refuses to fit into any category, ally itself with any adjective. She tilts her head at a peculiar angle, like a satellite dish.

"Don't you want to ask about Gerald?" Christy prompts.

"Gerald Bell? What about him?"

"Nothing." I feel terribly wrong, doing this. And yet, I scold, just forty minutes ago, in the recovery room, I was filled with steely determination, calling myself Superwoman. "You did mention, in the car that night, something about a family tree?"

"Living ordinances, yes. Gerald is considering conversion to the LDS faith, in which case he would want his ancestors to be baptized. Why? Are you also interested in learning about—?"

"Gerald's my brother," I interrupt. "I'm sorry we didn't tell you earlier. Don't blame him. It was my fault. It was a cruel thing to do, though."

She laughs.

"That explains a lot. You two seemed to know each other so well. I could tell there was something between you, but it wasn't any kind of . . . electricity. I couldn't figure out what was going on."

"Miss Kara here is a mystery to many," Christy comments.

At that point, I give a little cry. It is not serious, just a twinge, a cramp. But of course everything is magnified by what I just went through, not only physical sensations, but emotions, too.

"What?" Christy asks, suddenly alert.

"Nothing."

"How severe is the pain?"

"It's not even pain. Stop being such a mother."

"But I *am* a mother." She seems irritated by her own concern. "Where are those pills?"

I was given a sample packet, along with a prescription in case things got bad. I do not want to take them, but Christy insists. She goes back to the stand for water.

"She's kind of a nut," I apologize, "but her heart's in the right place. I hope she didn't get you in trouble. She knew I wasn't looking forward to getting this tooth out, so she thought she'd surprise me by finding you."

"I heard," Amy says. "I heard those people at the clinic."

"What people?"

"The ones shouting."

"I didn't. When people hold to irrational propositions I tend not to notice."

"I'm blind, but I'm not an idiot, or a child. You don't have to lie to me about having an abortion."

We sit. I look out over the river.

"What are you doing?" she asks.

"Shivering."

"Here." She gives me the least attractive sweater ever knitted, a green cardigan with big plastic buttons. "Gerald already has a record of his ancestry. The Family History Center was able to trace his people back several generations. We received it last week and passed it on."

"Did it have locations? Like where our father's family lived?"

"I wouldn't know that, of course. Someone else at the center looked it over. But they usually do. Why?"

I tell her. I tell her everything. She thinks about it. At least I think she thinks about it. Never having seen commonplace expressions, the muscles of her face do not have any guide. Either that or she is remarkably self-controlled.

"You should join us," she concludes.

"Why? Do you get some kind of Girl Scout pin if I do?"

"Because you're being tested."

"I'm good at tests."

"Because we can help. Because you're going through some terrible things."

"Not really. I haven't had a 'spell' in a few weeks now. I'm on the mend."

"If you join us, you'll go to heaven."

"You believe that?"

"I know it."

Her flat affect is very convincing. She drank in belief along with mother's milk, giving her a creepily persuasive certainty.

"What about you and Gerald?"

"What about us?"

"He's got a thing for you. You know it."

"Sometimes people confuse religious feelings with the other kind."

"How do *you* feel?"

She acts like she does not hear. She would be good at poker.

Christy returns, and I take a pill.

"Both," she orders.

"But it says, 'Take one, and if pain persists—'"

"Take both."

She waits, an orderly at a psychiatric institution, until I swallow.

"There is no reason to be in pain. I hate people who like to suffer."

"I was just telling Kara that she should consider attending more of our meetings for those interested in conversion."

Christy eyes us both, noting the sweater I have taken.

"Well, she'd certainly pass the dress code. What about me? You think I'd make a good LDSer?"

"All are welcome."

"What a hoot! Did you see the look on her face?"

"I don't think she has looks on her face."

"I'm tempted to join their crackpot religion. I bet I could move up through the ranks really fast, if she's any example of who they've got working for them. What do you become? A bishop?"

"They don't let women become anything."

"Well, I'd change that."

The pills are doing their work. Or maybe it is the long day, or the road. It keeps ribboning in front of us. I try fixing my eyes on a specific section, but it always passes, slips underneath, like a yanked tablecloth.

"So if Gerald already has the information, why hasn't he passed it on to you? He must know it's important. Hell, it's why you're here."

"Why I'm here," I echo.

Once, Christy and I were sitting around the kitchen table with Mother, and Christy, whether from genuine curiosity or a desire to shock, asked how a baby could get pushed through your vagina and not leave it "all saggy, like something that's lost its elastic?" I almost died. But Mother, with whom I had discussed nothing concerning sex except its general inadvisability, was surprisingly practical and informative. "The tissue reassembles itself," she said, "just like it was. There's nothing to worry about. Not on that score."

"So what do you think he sees in her?"

"Beats me," I shrug.

"Some guys like that whole girl-who-isn't-there thing."

"I don't think he's considering religious conversion just to get in her pants."

"That would make more sense than doing it because he believes in a God who lives on the planet Kolob."

"Where?"

"That's where He's at, according to them. It says so right here." She holds up a pamphlet. "I was reading it while you and her were having your soulful conversation."

"We weren't having a soulful conversation."

"You better watch it. She's got her eyes on you. I can tell."

"She doesn't have eyes."

"Probably does," Christy riffs, yawning into the night. "It's probably just an act, that 'Oh, I bumped into the table' bit. To lure in the unsuspecting."

"I can't believe you stole a pamphlet."

"I didn't steal it. That's why they're there, to be taken."

"I suppose."

"Anyway, we had a good time, didn't we?"

"Best abortion ever." I curl up, resting against her thigh. "Thank you."

She puts her hand on my head. She would run her fingers through my hair if only I had enough. I can feel the tires on the road and remember my resolution to take her away from all this, like a pirate swooping in on a rope, carrying off the fair-haired maiden. The pills are allowing my mind to expand beyond its natural borders.

"I could care for you," I murmur. "I could make you happy."

"That's a nice thing to say."

"I could fill you up."

"Beg pardon?"

". . . so that you would have difficulty *containing* me. In the military sense."

"I have no idea what you're talking about. You feel all right?"

"I mean, why drink five glasses of Long Island Iced Tea when you can have the real thing?"

Her fingers tense for just an instant.

Have I been speaking out loud, I wonder, or is she, in fact, the blind one, reading my thoughts through braille?

"Sleep," her voice comes from far away. "Sleep, baby girl."

I do not let her bring me home. I insist she go back to her place.

"I'll walk from here."

"Walk? You can barely put one foot in front of the other."

"No. I need this. I need some transition time." I gather what I have been given by the clinic, prescriptions, instructions, hot-line numbers, Frequently Asked Questions. I am dying to throw it all away. "This was the nicest thing anyone has ever done for me."

"Let me take you back to your mamma. You're not yourself."

"I feel great."

I do. I am. I have crested an invisible peak and am walking more easily. Gravity is on my side.

"Now, if anyone wants to know," I coach, "we were just out all day having a great time."

"Isn't that the truth?" she asks, with her usual mix of innocence and insinuation.

I do not go home. I am too happy. I hover, by the light of a nearly full moon, down the path that leads to the creek.

What I want to do—what I *will* do, since everything is now possible—is tell A.C. He is the only one who can begin to understand. Also, I want to throw in his face all that stuff he told me about my feelings for Christy not being real. The creek here is at its fastest, just before widening out. Moonlight rushes away, being taken somewhere. I empty my pockets of all the "literature," superstitiously rip it up and set the confetti afloat.

Abortion is murder. Maybe this is what a murderer feels, freed from the prohibitions of Society.

Or maybe you are pleasantly, deliriously out of control, the more prudent part of my mind cautions.

The Bait Shop is dark, which surprises me. It is not late, maybe ten thirty. Usually, Horace is here, holding court with all the Creekside men his age. They sit and smoke. Or chew. Play cards and tell stories. Sometimes, waiting for A.C., I would listen. But none of them are here now. The freezer chest hums. He is on the road, I realize. Hauling for his friend. I hop down off the porch and begin to circle the house, though that is the wrong word. It is not geometrically regular enough to encircle. I follow where it unexpectedly juts and where tiny ravines form between walls that, in some cases, almost touch. What I am looking for is simple enough: a way in.

"Hello?" I call, but not loud enough to be heard, more like a bat, checking the acoustics of the place.

The pines, which grow thick once you get away from the creek, shut out the moon.

Finally, a light appears, dim and faint. I make my way to a sill that, as I grip, allows my fingers to sink in. Through the glass I see their kitchen, a fantastic jumble of cans, bottles, and boxes on shelves rising high, so high you would need a chair or ladder to reach the top ones, and a big table in similar disarray, covered by papers, piles of gear, and what looks like dirty laundry. Mae is sitting there. My heart takes the little skip it always does when I see her. I am about to tap on the windowpane, but her expression is serious, as if she is in the middle of an act that requires the utmost concentration. She is frowning, fiddling with a device in her hand. She works it again and a flame appears. It is a lighter. She hunches so it illuminates only her face and the bowl of the familiar glass pipe she is heating. I watch, along with her, the vapors appear and travel through the tube. I am only a few feet away, scared of being seen, but at the same time know that nothing will distract her attention. She waits until the pipe is thick with fumes, then sucks them all in.

CHAPTER TEN

"I'm working now. Don't get me flustered."

"Just trying to have a conversation."

"Well, this is not the place to do it."

Maybe so, but I do not know where to get Delilah alone. The Best Steakhouse in Witch's Falls is surprisingly busy for a Tuesday night.

"How'd you get here, anyway?" she asks.

"My old bike, from high school."

"Your bike?"

I can see it becoming another kooky Kara story. She rode all the way to The Best, on her bicycle!

"It's not at home. I checked his room. It would be a big bunch of papers, maybe a chart, too. In an envelope from the LDS Outreach Center in Little Rock."

"I don't know nothing about that. Are you ready to order?"

"I'll have the garden salad."

"Salad?" Her pen hesitates, unsure how to form such an alien word. "Blue cheese dressing?"

"Just oil and vinegar."

149

"That's clear," she warns, as if I might not be getting my minimum daily requirement of cholesterol.

"Come on, Delilah. Nobody knows Gerald like you. Are you telling me you haven't see it? A big old family tree?"

"He warned me you might come around snooping like this. Asking questions."

"When did he say that? After he got it in the mail?"

"Yes. No. I mean, I don't want to talk to you."

She goes off.

The crowd here is mostly middle-aged, all taking the place's name literally, ordering gray cuts of meat that come with coleslaw in a cup and a foil-wrapped potato. But perhaps I am being too critical. It is the best steakhouse in Witch's Falls, by virtue of there being no other. I admire how Delilah interacts with the customers, people she knows socially but to whom she is now momentarily subservient. Such a conflict would reduce me to extreme awkwardness. How familiar to act? How groveling and falsely ingratiating? How angry and resentful? She feels none of this. I envy her ease, how she writes down their orders as if doing them a favor, an easy one that requires no thanks or compensation.

She returns with a lettuce-lined bowl full of tomato, green pepper, and still-frozen artichoke hearts.

"I don't understand. If he got it, why didn't he tell me? He knows I need to see it."

"He said it was just making you crazy, this stuff."

"Crazy? I'll show him who's crazy."

"See? When you talk that way, people naturally assume—"

"You know what quid pro quo is?"

Her eyes widen.

"It's not a food item. It means— Never mind. Listen, I am willing to do something for you if you tell me where those papers are."

"Do something like what?"

"Mother's having a dinner party next week. Well, not a party, but it's a formal affair. To introduce us to someone. Officially. Didn't Gerald tell you?"

"No," she frowns.

"Course not. Because he wasn't going to bring you. But I could invite you."

"You? Why?"

"I told you, because . . ." I sigh. It is like trying to conspire with an inanimate object. "If you tell me where those papers are—"

"I got to go," she says, focusing on another table. "I'll be right back."

She is wearing a vaguely cowgirlish uniform with an apron that ties in a big bow. I visualize the tiger tattoo he framed so perfectly between her shoulder blades. Which she then threatened to have removed. I suppose in her eyes it was like an engagement ring. And he had done something to betray her. But they are still together, so just what is going on?

"Well, well, look who's here."

Dr. Macatee and his wife are standing before me. I recognize her from the picture I saw in his office. She does bear a striking resemblance to an elk. I wonder if that is why he married her.

"Glad to see you're eating healthy," he says.

". . . for two," I babble inanely, wondering if I can kick *myself* under the table, to cure me of this mindless instinct to please, to please the wrong people, those who are not my friends.

"You going to be in town much longer?"

"I don't think so."

"What are you doing the rest of the summer, dear?" Mrs. M. asks.

"I thought I might go on a little bit of a trip," I improvise.

"Isn't that nice?"

"Good to get around while you can," he smiles, envisioning me safely strapped down with a screaming child and all the killing financial, emotional, and physical demands that brings.

151

But the joke is on you, Dr. Female Hysteria, I think, moodily chewing on a piece of carrot. You can kiss my purple vagina.

"I can't stay long." Delilah sits opposite me. "I'm not supposed to be doing this, but I told my boss it's a family emergency. Now what is this dinner party about?"

"I'm not sure I'm allowed to say." I try to sound mysterious. "There's someone she wants us to meet. I think it's someone she's been seeing."

"You mean a man?"

"Yes."

"I can't believe Gerald didn't tell me about this."

"He's had a lot on his mind, lately, I gather, what with this new interest in genealogy and stuff."

"LDS," she says gruffly. "I know all about it. That blind cunt."

I almost drop my fork.

"He tried to get me to come to one of those meetings. I told him, Hell no. I already work in one of these places. I sure don't need to worship here."

"Is that why you want him to leave Witch's Falls and go west?"

"Partly. But mostly I just feel it's time. He's still kind of tied to your mother's apron strings, if you'll pardon me for saying so."

"And you'd rather he be tied to yours?"

"Jerr and me are *good*," she says, like it's the daily special, one she's truly recommending. "Now, when is this dinner? If Jean's bringing home a man, I want to be there. That might just be the motivation Gerald needs."

"Next Friday."

"I'll get the night off."

"Wait. You got to hold up your end of the deal. Where's those papers?"

"At the parlor. He put them in the desk drawer. The one out front."

"Can you get them for me?"

"No. That would be dishonest. I've already told you more than I should. You figure out how to get hold of them. And if you get caught, don't you dare mention me, or the only philosophy you'll be studying is how to close up that new asshole I tore you."

"Yes ma'am."

I must admit, I am impressed. I can almost see her being my sister-in-law. Then she turns all moody.

"I knew he had a thing for that girl. I could tell the minute I saw them together. I don't know why. She dresses like carpeting."

"I think it's more of a spiritual connection."

"I'm spiritual!"

"Yes, you are."

"I'd scratch her eyes out, but it wouldn't do any good."

"No," I sympathize. "In this case, it wouldn't."

"You think I should bring wine?"

"Where?"

"To your mother's, for dinner. It's the first time we'll really be sitting down together. You think I should bring a bottle of red wine? I want to make a good impression."

"Oh, you'll make a fine impression."

"Thank you, Kara." She leans across the table and kisses me on the cheek. "I never believed half the things they said about you."

Why *is* Mother having this dinner party? I ask myself. Getting caught that night in the office seems to have made her reconsider her situation. She must have talked to Coach Kip and decided it was time to come clean, at least with her family. The result shows what pressure she was under. Her mood, now, is so much more upbeat. She no longer goes around with that phony, nervous smile like she did before. I miss it. It gave me something to push against. Instead, she is happy all the time, which I am glad about, of course, glad for her, but not quite sure what role there is left for me to play, now that Tormentor is no longer available.

"A roast?" she proposes.

"Kind of hot for that."

"You know, you're right. The thing is, I don't want to be in the kitchen doing last minute preparations. I want to be out here with the rest of you."

"You could serve something already prepared. Like a fancy chicken salad, maybe. With asparagus."

"Why, Kara, that is a brilliant idea. Sort of like an indoor picnic. I mean, why do we have to be so stiff and formal? After all, the point of this is to have fun, isn't it?"

"Is it?"

"I'm so glad we can have conversations like this. You're going to make someone very happy, someday."

She gives my shoulder an affectionate squeeze as she passes into the kitchen.

Is that an insult? I ask myself. ". . . make someone very happy." It certainly sounds like an insult, but I cannot quite figure out how to turn it into one.

The phone rings.

"Why, yes," she says. "Of course."

The sad fact is, she is just being nice.

"Kara, it's your doctor."

"Macatee?"

"No. That man up North."

She does not even imply, as she surely would have before, that he is a half-caste, mail-order-degree, coffee-colored con-man. Is this what adult love does? I consider, going upstairs to talk in the hall-way. Turn you into a pod person, a parody of a Decent Human Being? I had always pictured love as a warping or deranging factor, a type of disfigurement. Where do these assumptions come from?

"Kara? My records show we have not spoken in several weeks."

"I know. I am sorry, Dr. Vallomthail."

"When you last called, you were quite upset. It was from some type of store."

"Yes."

"The . . ."

I can see him squinting at his notes.

"Pig and Toad?" he reads doubtfully.

"Pik'n Tote. I'm surprised you wrote that down. I apologize for not being in touch. It has been somewhat active here."

"Did you confirm the fact that you are pregnant?"

"No! I mean, yes. I confirmed that I was not. That problem has been resolved."

"Been resolved successfully?"

"From my point of view, yes. I am no longer," I look around, "in that way."

"Then we are back to where we were before."

"No. Somewhat further along. I believe I am going to be able to track down a bunch of collateral relatives."

"You are still pursuing the possibility of a bone marrow transplant then?"

"It's my best option, isn't it?"

"Medically, yes. But I do not want you pinning all your hopes on what could turn out to be a wild goose."

"Or a pig in a poke."

"People greatly underestimate the psychological toll cancer takes on a patient. I am concerned about your state of mind."

"My mind was never better. I am thinking with a newfound clarity. In fact, I may be on the verge of solving this entire problem."

"As I explained before, the most commonsensical approach is simply to wait and see."

"'Common sense' is an oxymoron."

"A—?"

"Besides, don't you hear what I'm saying? I think I have discovered a long-lost branch of the family. I should know more, in a few days."

"Very well. I do wish you would return to the city so I could examine you." I hear him speaking to someone else. "Just a moment. My receptionist would like to confirm an aspect of record keeping with you. Take care, Kara."

There is a familiar beep, and I am talking to Esther.

"He called," she says. "A man. Looking for you."

"Who?"

"A Professor Lewisohn?"

Saul.

"He said you'd left no forwarding information. I didn't know what to tell him."

"You didn't say I was here, did you?"

"No. That's confidential."

"Good."

"But I thought you'd want to know. He sounded . . ." Her paint-scraper voice, usually so assertive, goes soft, "concerned, I guess."

Concerned about what? I wonder. About a lawsuit? About filling my fellowship in case I die? Or concerned—this would be the most alarming scenario of all—out of genuine feeling?

It really is a violation, I fume, later that evening, much more so than what he did to my person, his trying to track me down, asserting some kind of paternal, conjugal, professorial authority where none exists! I see I have failed twice to fit my foot through the pant leg of my maroon-striped jeans. I am getting all worked up about nothing, as usual. The important thing is to dress in dark colors. Unfortunately, the only black bag I own is a huge shoulder strap number Mother foisted on me several years ago. It could hold an entire lending library besides the notebook, pen, and flashlight I put in. At the last minute, I add the purloined latex gloves. Our crowbar, from the garage, is already hidden in some bushes out front.

Mother is off having middle-aged sex with her boyfriend. Gerald, amazingly, is home. The light is on under his door. I tiptoe past, hoping not to hear him practicing prayers in some bizarre Utah-based language.

Why is everyone so weird? I complain. How is it that, despite my strenuous attempts to defy convention, I alone am left to define *normal*?

With that thought, I go off to break into the tattoo parlor.

"We're going to do what?" A.C. asks, when I meet him around the corner from the shop's back door.

"You heard me. There's stuff in there I've got to see. And he hasn't offered to show it to me. He feels it just feeds my obsession. Well, I'm not asking anyone for anything anymore. I take what's mine."

"But it isn't yours. That's why you're breaking in, right?"

"Technically. But there's no way we'll get in trouble. Even if we get caught, which we won't, Gerald would never press charges."

"Then what am I doing here?"

"I don't really know how to break into a place," I confess. "But I brought this."

I haul out the crowbar.

"Oh, and you think that, because of what I do, I know all about busting through doors and stuff."

"Well, yes. I also wanted to talk, and knew if I said what I really had in mind you might not come."

"If you wanted to talk, we could always meet for a cup of coffee. Talk doesn't have to involve following someone all the way to Booneville or committing a class C felony."

"Coffee?" I make a face. "See, that's the problem. I don't want to drink a cup of coffee with you, and you don't want to get high with me."

"I'm not sixteen anymore."

"No, you're not." I stare significantly at his exposed electric-pink boxers. "Look, the stuff in there is important to me. I could really use your help. Plus, doing things like this together kind of reminds me of how it used to be with us. Don't you remember?"

". . . never thought *I'd* turn out to be the grown-up," he mutters, taking the crowbar.

"Wait." I burrow into the bag and come out with the gloves. "So we won't leave fingerprints."

We both put them on. It is like preparing for surgery.

"I went by your place the other night," I whisper. "Nobody there."

"Horace is on the road."

"I figured. How's your mamma?"

"Fine," he says, with a little too much edge. "Why?"

"No reason."

The back door does not have a roll-down gate or a grille. I shine the light.

"She can't stop talking about you," he goes on. "It's like you're the daughter she never had."

"I thought that was you."

"One of these days that mouth of yours is going to get you in a pile of trouble. This bolt," he pronounces, handing back the crowbar, "is not fit to secure a chicken coop."

"That's good, right?"

He takes off his wire-rimmed glasses, straightens out a side piece, and works the end into the keyhole.

"It's very racist, you just assuming I know how to do this."

"But you do, apparently."

". . . still racist."

"Doesn't this feel like old times? Being kids again?"

"I like the gloves," he admits. "Where'd you get 'em?"

"You don't want to know."

"No, I suppose I don't."

There is a click.

"Quick," he says.

We are in the back, where the electric needle apparatus looms. I shine the light over two chairs, one for Gerald and one for the customer. It is surprisingly stark. I had expected something a little more high-tech.

"The desk is out front."

"You don't want that light to shine through the window."

I turn it off. In the dark, we shuffle, feeling our way. The crowbar, weighing down the bag, clunks against my side. Not being able to see makes it easier to talk, to broach certain subjects.

"She must be lonely, with Horace gone."

"Mae? Going to get worse before it gets better."

"What's that supposed to mean?"

"Things are getting hot for me, too. I may have to disappear a while myself."

"Where would you go?"

"I don't know. But it wouldn't be the worst thing in the world. Look at you. You got away."

"Did I? Damn!"

"That's one way to find what you're looking for," he says dryly, as I bend over to rub my leg.

The desk is right in front of us. Before I can open the drawer, though, a patrol car goes by, slow. Without hesitation, we duck down, knocking against each other as we crouch to the floor. The lights linger, stretching the shadows.

"—don't suppose you have any more of that crystal on you?" I breathe, clutching his arm.

159

"Going to be fine," he assures me. "Just so you know, that's my hand you're stepping on."

"Sorry."

They begin to move again. Our breath returns.

"And another thing," I whisper, still on the floor, "you were wrong about Christy Lee. She's much more real than we used to give her credit for."

"In what way?"

"I don't know. No way in particular. But she and I have had a few really good talks since I came back."

"Is that what you got me down here for? To tell me Christy Lee has your best interests at heart?"

"Maybe." I am glad the dark conceals my silly grin. "I didn't want you to think you were the only one capable of finding true love."

"I never said I found true love."

"What's his name again? Something unusual, right? Hey, how can you be talking about leaving when you've found your soul mate?"

"He's not my soul mate. I didn't—"

"And what about your mother? She'll be here all alone."

"Are those papers in there? Because I don't want to spend the next three years picking cotton at the Cummins Correctional Facility."

I cover the light with my hand so it is just a red glow. They are right on top, in one of those unrippable plastic envelopes.

"This is it! Look!"

"I don't have to look. You look. You get what you need, and then let's go."

There are pages of background information, but I am not interested in that. Not right now. I unfold a much larger sheet. It is a chart, with many lines. Our family tree.

"See? Right here. We've got two uncles and an aunt! In Shreveport! And they've got children. It even gives the addresses. Cousins."

My heart is pounding. I shake my head at everyone's small-town yokel faith in conspiracies of silence. Here, despite their stubborn resistance, is Truth. Now all I have to do is steal a car, drive to Louisiana, confront my newfound kin, and force them, at gunpoint, to submit to testing.

"You OK?" A.C. asks.

I am writing slowly, legibly, carefully transcribing names and contact information, but strange sounds are issuing from my mouth, a kind of hoarse panting. Hyperventilation, I recognize, from too much adrenalin.

"I'm fine."

"Let's get the hell out of here."

"Wait."

I put the papers away, carefully setting them as they were, so he won't know I have been here. In doing so, I uncover the flashlight. It happens to shine on my favorite of Gerald's recent designs, that wave he has tacked to the wall, a blue-green curl, caught, arrested in time yet somehow alive, aching to break.

"Isn't that beautiful?"

"I wouldn't know."

"You ever seen the ocean?"

"I been to Galveston."

"That's the Gulf."

He takes the flashlight and turns it off. Then he pushes me out, guiding me past the furniture and equipment. The door shuts behind us. It is as if we had never been inside. Our sins are erased. I look at A.C. He is smiling. Older, I see now for the first time, significantly older, but still smiling.

"You really leaving Witch's Falls?" I ask.

"Aren't you?"

"Yeah, but . . ."

". . . thought I'd stay forever? Become part of the scenery?"

"No. I mean, maybe. But what about your mamma?"

"She'll get by. Or not."

"That's pretty cold."

"Things are bad."

"Seem just the same, to me."

"Only in your head."

"Well, that's where I mostly live."

"This was fun," he concludes, handing me the flashlight, "but I'm not doing stuff like this with you anymore, ever again."

"Ever?"

"Don't come looking for me," he instructs. "Don't call. I won't be answering. That won't be my number. And don't you go asking about me. It wouldn't be a good idea. For you."

"Why? Just how much trouble are you in?"

"I'm not in any trouble. Yet. It's just time, that's all." He peels the gloves off and lets them drop to the ground. "Stay away from the shop too."

"What about Mae?"

"Like I said, this was fun."

He puts his hands—the hands I love—on either side of my face and kisses me. It is such a swift, unexpected gesture that I do not have time to react, or even be sure, immediately after, it really happened.

CHAPTER ELEVEN

Anthony Bell. Caroline Gomez. (I wonder what the story is behind that marriage.) Alice Bell. Spinster? Maiden aunt? Or, I try to contain my excitement, perhaps my direct ancestress, romance-wise. I am beside myself with anticipation. But another voice keeps warning, Calm down. This has to be handled just right. A call, out of the blue, from some nut-job Arkansan trying to interest them in providing a DNA sample, could ruin everything right from the start. First impressions are crucial. I need a new wardrobe. Something more along the lines of an Avon lady or Bible salesman. I need a whole new manner of speaking, less honest and forthright. What I really need is a stunt double to deal with these people, because I do not see myself as the tearful reunion type. Looking at it from their point of view, I probably do not come across as anyone's vision of a long-lost niece or cousin. Barring a complete personality makeover, what I could use is a sidekick, someone better at talking their way into people's homes, into their bloodstreams, and finally into their stem cells.

"You want sprinkles with that?"

"I surely do," I try gushing in my best Miss Congeniality manner.

I regress, go back to the gazebo, the setting for all those child-hood rites of passage in which I never participated, trying to lick an ice cream cone into shape before it melts all over my wrist.

Part of Mother's attempt to create a time-free replica of my room was leaving a packet of old report cards, bound by a ribbon, on top of my dresser. I did not get around to looking at them until last night, when one caught my eye. Now, I fish it from my pocket. It has the usual column of A's, to each of which someone has very carefully appended "-hole." Though I have no memory of this, I recognize the rounded, textbook penmanship. Only one girl writes like this.

It is Christy, of course, who will come with me to Shreveport and beyond, who will save my life.

"That looks good."

I hastily stuff the card back in my pocket.

"It is."

"I wouldn't have figured you for the sprinkle-type."

"What type is that?"

"Well," Coach Kip is standing outside the gazebo as if waiting to be invited in, "they all taste the same, don't they? I mean, if you closed your eyes, could you tell the green ones, from, say, the black?"

"Brown," I correct. "Green is mint, I suppose. Brown represents chocolate."

"But does it taste like chocolate?"

"No more than this strawberry ice cream tastes much like straw-berries," I shrug.

He is heavy and sweating, wearing a shirt and tie, trousers in-stead of sweatpants.

"I saw you from across the street," he explains.

"How come you're all dressed up?"

"Been to see the lawyers."

He steps inside. Normal clothes do not do him justice. They di-minish his attributes, the cave-man robustness Mother goes for.

"I'm more of a hot fudge man, myself."

I struggle and fail to come up with an innocuous reply, or to make eye contact. I am acting, I know, like a bitch, but cannot help it.

"They got a language all their own, these attorneys," he sighs, settling onto one of the planks that line the inside of the octagon. "I sure do miss my daughter."

"What's her name?"

"Alexandra."

"That's a nice name."

"She hated it here," he says frankly. "Still does. So that's kind of a stumbling block to these visits we're discussing."

"You could go see her."

"I could. But school vacations are when we get a lot of our work in, team-wise."

"Oh, that's right." I remember the pep rally. Seeing Gerald with Amy for the first time. Getting high with Corinne and her friends under the bleachers. That seems a long time ago. "They say you're an 'offensive genius.'"

He smiles.

"I've heard tell that's what you are. A genius, I mean. On all those tests."

"I can't stand that word."

"Why?"

"It's lost its meaning. It used to be this spirit that accompanied you everywhere and kind of buzzed by your ear—like a dragonfly, I always pictured—looking out for you, telling you what to do in any situation. Your *genius*. Everybody had one. Plato called them 'daemons,' which got mistranslated as 'demons,' thus acquiring a false, negative connotation."

"Pre-Socratic philosophy is tempting but doesn't really lead anywhere," he ponders. "It's like trying to form building blocks out of sand. You can't put one on top of the other. They always just collapse down into themselves. *If A, then A*, is the best you can come up with."

I blink. It is like before, when I saw him address the crowd. He is saying something completely different, which I monitor on an alternate frequency, but meanwhile ventriloquize a separate train of thought, some random speculation about Heraclitus and company.

"—never want to get between you two. I know how important a mother-daughter relationship is."

"But you must hate her," I say. "Your wife, I mean, if you're having such a fight over your daughter."

"I don't hate her."

"Then why aren't you still together?"

"Love isn't the absence of hate."

I redouble my focus, trying to make sure this is what he is actually saying, and not some substitution my mind is making while he spouts platitudes.

"Well, isn't it, kind of? I mean, the way I see it, we exist in a medium of love, like fish in the ocean, so we don't normally recognize it. It takes a violent negation, like hate, to make us understand love, in our lives, to make it stand apart from . . . this rocking current that's almost part of our metabolism."

"—think you're making a mess of things," he points out.

"Damn."

I switch the cone to my other hand and start licking my forearm. Some of the melted ice cream has pooled in the crook of my elbow. It is disgusting. And, of course, I look like an idiot.

"All I'm trying to say is, I know it was a shock, finding out about your mother and me the way you did, but I hope we can get past that, as a family."

"No problemo." I ineffectually rub my palm against my shorts. The stickiness remains. "I'm going to be out of here soon, anyway."

"Are you?"

"Yup. Back to school, with a side trip first. I understand about your daughter not wanting to come down here on vacations, but you tell her it's probably not as bad as she makes out. *I* hated it. Once upon a time."

"And now you don't?"

"Well," I think of the report card snuggled safely in my back pocket, "like I said, it has made me more aware of love."

"You're a lot like her."

"Who?"

"Jean. Your mother. The way you talk."

"I am not. We're nothing alike."

"How she slights herself," he elaborates, ignoring my objection. "Pretends she's not special, when she is. I tell her, You're hiding yourself under a bushel."

"Her light. Hiding her light under a bushel."

"Exactly. Same as you saying you hate the word *genius*. What's wrong with being a genius?"

"Geniuses don't sit in the middle of Witch's Falls, Arkansas, letting ice cream run down their leg."

"I've coached boys like you. All the natural ability in the world but when they've got their four, five, six yards, they go to the ground. Or step out of bounds. They don't take the hit."

I watch him straighten his spine as he goes into locker-room mode.

"They are afraid to go to the next level!"

"Pretty nice view up here already." I meet his gaze unblinkingly. "If I went any higher, I might have trouble conducting simple conversations."

"This dinner, you think I should bring a bottle of wine?"

I stuff the rest of the scoop in my mouth so I will not have to answer. Since when did I become the world's authority in matters of dining etiquette?

"The thing is, I'm a guest, yes. But it's kind of like your mother and I are appearing in public for the first time as a couple. So in that sense, I'm hosting, along with her. In which case she might be offended if I brought something. Like I'm not acknowledging the fact of what we already are. Like I'm just some gentleman caller."

"So *we're* the guests?" I literally splutter, spraying fragments of cone. "Gerald and me? In our own house?"

"Well, no. Of course not. You're more like witnesses, I suppose. To our new status."

"I've already been a witness, remember? In her back office? And let me tell you, that is one picture I am having a lot of trouble erasing from my mind."

"Your mother and I are in love," he says. "That ocean you were taking about? It's inside us."

It is a simple plan. Christy and I will take off in her car. Another "girls' day out," like before. Except this one will be overnight. Or maybe a few days. Enough for us to go to Shreveport, Louisiana, ingratiate ourselves with my daddy's relatives, and sweet-talk them into providing cheek swabs for the national registry. Who knows how long that will take? We can stay in a motel. And from there . . .

For once let us not speculate in such detail, I counsel my rampant and surprisingly pornographic imagination. Let us just take it as far as Christy/DNA/motel. A mix of business and pleasure. If what it leads to is continuing on up North, somewhat in the nature of an elopement, or maybe just her wanting to see the big city for an extended period of time, so be it.

I walk slowly, taking my time.

When we swam, I must have brushed against a bush that was swarming with ticks. I completely freaked out. Christy, on the other hand, was fascinated, and kept finding more—"Look, here's another"—like they formed a pattern or constellation.

"Just get 'em off!"

"I can't. If you leave the head in it swells up. You know that. You'll be itching for weeks. Plus, it's unsightly."

"Not as unsightly as having these gross things suck my blood. How come you didn't get any?"

"I never get ticks." She shook her head like it was a regret. "They don't like me."

It was true. She never got bit by mosquitoes either. There was something about her skin. An imperviousness.

"Here's one more." She lifted my arm. I submitted like I was a rag doll. "How did it get all the way under there?"

"My mother says you can use oil, that it suffocates them so they have to pull their head out."

"Ain't got no oil here, sister."

She was clearly enjoying herself. We were at an isolated stretch of the creek on a very hot summer day. I was in a one-piece bathing suit. She, of course, disdained such encumbrances, stripping down to her underwear. I had no clue, at the time, as to my feelings, as to how they might influence my actions. I was brilliantly stupid. No one could have been more ignorant, as if my very life depended on it.

"What are we going to do?"

She went through her bag and got out a pack of cigarettes.

"Oh, well, that's just great. I've got these little bastards burrowing deeper and deeper into my flesh and you have yourself a smoke."

"Shh." She took one puff and began to hover with the glowing tip. "The trick is for you to stay absolutely still."

"Wait a minute. You're not going to—"

She brought the red-hot ember a micron away from one of the specks. I began to feel my skin sear.

"Christy . . ."

"Look!"

Lo and behold, the dot transformed itself into a hideous eight-legged tick, raising its head as if my epidermis was not solid at all, more like the surface of a pond. She tapped its back with the cigarette. We both watched it shrivel to nothing, then give up a tiny puff of vapor.

"That is so cool!" she exulted.

"But now I'm scarred for life."

"No way. See?" She brushed the corpse aside. It was true. There was no mark at all. "Now, let's get the rest of these suckers."

"That's OK. I can just wait until I get home. My mother will—"

"Don't move a muscle," she instructed, taking a deep drag to stoke the fire again.

I watched the top of her head as it moved methodically over my body. I liked it that she was so intent. It gave me license to stare unabashedly for the first time. Brazenly. Lustfully, if I had known such a feeling was even possible, much less permissible. But can you stare lustfully at a person's head? I could. It was the only head I had ever coveted. And of course—"Don't move," she kept repeating, which was fine with me—all my feeling flowed from being ordered to remain passive and helpless while some awful procedure was performed on me, a transforming, purifying ritual.

"You are Tick City."

She pushed up the bottom of my bathing suit.

But nothing happened. I mean everything happened, in my head and heart, but only later, lying in bed that night, did I consider, oh so tentatively, the sexual implications of what had taken place. And even that was more marveling at how, by a series of coincidences, it had mimicked, in so many outward particulars, what I imagined a scene of passion might resemble.

"Nothing happened," I repeat, standing, now, before her house.

She did not leave a single mark. By the end, I was a statue, incapable of even breathing. Yet I recall noticing, while she investigated with the single-mindedness of a bloodhound every possible nook or cranny a tick could wedge itself into, that I had never seen her more interested in what she was doing, more alive. Her impervious skin *glowed*.

I press the doorbell. Inside, a baby is crying.

"Come in!" she calls.

It is a heavy door. The way it closes makes you feel like you are entering a submarine or some other sealed vessel. The outside world falls away. The baby's crying, however, does not. He is wailing.

"In the kitchen," she calls.

I wade through soft carpeting. I have not yet spent time on the ground floor, only upstairs and down. The living room and dining area owe less to plantation-era civility than prime-time TV soap operas. Shiny glass-and-metal furniture sits under smeary paintings of Nature. The kitchen, with its new appliances and acres of granite countertop on which you can tell no home-cooked meal has ever been prepared, reverberates with Shelby's outraged shrieks.

It is the tiles, I remind myself, trying to cover my ears. Their harsh echo makes a bad sound worse.

"What are you trying to do," I joke, coming up on her from behind, "strangle him?"

Then I see it is not Christy but Ilene, holding Shelby in her arms. She has got a bottle, which he is not taking. Various strewn cookies and toys are evidence of nothing else working either.

"Hello, Kara," she smiles. "We are having a hissy fit."

"Oh . . . my." I try to instantly adjust my entire affect.

I am shocked that I could have mistaken her for Christy. They have absolutely nothing in common. Except all this, I reconsider, looking around.

"It's not always peaches and cream." She bounces the squalling tot on her knee. He shows no sign of gratitude. "You want to have a try?"

"What?" I shout back.

She somehow interprets this as "Yes," thrusting him over like I am a fully qualified member of the bomb squad.

"I have to go the little girls room. I'll be right back."

"Wait," I call, but all my attention is suddenly engulfed by the sheer force of this squirming, struggling wild child as he tries to work himself free of my grasp.

He almost succeeds. He gets airborne for about a half second before I catch him on his way to the floor.

"Oh no you don't. Quite the crybaby, aren't you? Where'd you get that from? Both your parents are pretty cool customers."

"I haaaaaate aaaaall of yooooo!" it seems to rasp in some prelinguistic mode of communication, gagging on its own bile.

"I know. I used to feel the same way. As you get older, you'll find—Will you be quiet, please? As you get older, you'll find—"

But he will not shut up. I forget what I am going to say, which is a great rarity, and understand, all at once without the usual intervening seventeen months of hell, just why it is mothers throw their children out windows. For some reason though, I am not mad. There is an odd check to my usual feelings of contempt.

"That's right. Cry." I try reverse psychology. "Go ahead. Get it out of your system. You'll feel better. I wish I'd cried more as a child."

That does not work either. I remember Christy's mindless credo.

"PACE! Positive Attitude Changes Everything."

Unfortunately, I have to scream to make myself understood over his amplified roar.

"Positive Attitude Changes Everything! You hear?"

Ilene chooses this moment to reenter the kitchen. She takes back the arching bundle, cooing:

"There, there."

"What the hell's he crying for?" I demand.

"I haven't the faintest idea. It could be gas. Do you need to burp, little man? Shelby need to make a burpy-wurpy?"

I can see her doing this to Martin, twenty-three years ago, talking the same way, ignoring his rage, which only enrages him more.

"I'm looking for Christy."

"Christy's not here. I don't know where she is. I thought she might be with you."

She almost winks.

"Any idea when she'll be back?"

"Now hush, child. Let me try putting him down."

The kitchen opens out onto the yard. There is a blow-up wading pool and a little playpen with netting for walls. She sets him down at the bottom of that and produces a lollipop. He grabs it with both hands.

"I shouldn't be doing this. Sugar's not good for them."

"You did right," I say bleakly, stunned by the sudden silence. "It was either him or us."

"Now, the answer to your question is no, I don't know when Christy is coming back. She often does this. She takes off, for the whole day. I don't know why. Or where. She just needs her space, I guess."

"Martin doesn't mind?"

"Martin is a very tolerant person. And busy," she adds significantly. "He has a number of civic obligations, in addition to keeping his normal office hours."

"Good thing they have you."

"Isn't it?" Her phone rings. "Will you excuse me, please?"

While she talks, I gaze at the greedy, demanding little personification of Will now working its gums over the lollipop. What would it be like, I wonder, to literally dissolve your mind in the tragedies and joys of such a primitive being? Not so bad, perhaps. This is, I know, leftover hormones talking, remnants of my brief pregnancy. But why not listen to what they have to say? They are part of me too.

"A floral tribute," she confirms. "Nothing too extravagant. That'll be just fine. Oh, I think 'Rest in Peace' will do."

Properties here extend much further back than on Bluebelle Road. When they do end, it is not to abut someone else's yard but in a tumbledown stone wall, remnant of some built-over farm. Beyond that, a secondary-growth forest rises, low trees and tamed wilderness.

"I apologize. Martin's father founded our local merchants association. As an honorary member, I take it upon myself to have flowers sent when one of our former colleagues is deceased."

"Someone died?" I ask, not really listening, trying to get my eyes to jump that wall. I am so turned around I cannot think what lies on the other side.

"John Robbins. You probably don't remember him. For many years he was the town's only butcher."

"Mr. Robbins? Out at the Home? Of course I know him."

"He passed away early this morning."

"I'm sorry to hear that."

Is it the creek, past the trees, and then down? Or does the wood clear after a few hundred yards, and you find yourself approaching the highway from a different direction? Or do you come instead to the hog farm? I remember a physics candidate describing to me how the universe does not end, but curves. Is that what it is like, having a child, realizing you are just one more section of an unimaginably all-encompassing circle?

"Of course now there are no more butchers. Just the meat counter out at the Walmart."

I wrench my attention away from the Infinite.

"Will you tell Christy that I came by?"

174

"Of course, dear. We're all looking forward to seeing you at the military reenactment."

"Oh yes."

She gazes fondly down at Shelby, as if addressing her infantilized son.

"Martin likes you so much."

"I like him too."

"He always says you're the one that got away."

"Beg pardon?"

"Michael, my late husband, was a very scholarly man. People don't know that about him. They associate him with real estate and building houses, but that was just something he did to provide for his family. At home, he had a whole study full of books."

"Did he?"

"He used to retire there in the evening. I think he intended, one day, to hand the business over to Martin and devote himself to the pursuit of knowledge full time. But it was not to be."

Not knowing what to say, I just sigh.

"I think you've had enough, sir."

She pulls the stick, extracting the lollipop from his slack jaw. He is pacified to the state where his eyes stare glassily past us, on up to the sky.

"Seems kind of boring, taking care of children."

"Oh, you have no idea. And so isolating. Mr. Casimir acted as if he couldn't change a diaper to save his life. As if it were beyond his skills. This was a man who worked construction from the time he was thirteen."

"You seem to have come through it pretty much unscathed."

"Well, I made a conscious decision, early on." She continues to fixate on the child, even though his pupils—I can see what Christy means, how disconcerting it is—completely bypass us, deny our corporeal existence. "Once, I had to go out for something, when

Martin was just about this age. It was an emergency but Mr. Casimir was home, so I left him on the floor with all his toys out and, naturally, gave my husband a bunch of instructions about where the bottle was, what to do if he had an accident, how he liked to be held . . . When I came back, two hours later, Martin was in the exact same spot as when I had left him. That man hadn't done a thing. Hadn't picked him up, hadn't played with him, hadn't fed him or changed him or even said hello. I could tell. His own son."

Then she does something odd. She starts to lick the saliva-coated, slicked-over lollipop she just took from her grandson's ruby-stained mouth.

"So when Martin had our little Shelby," she goes on, reliving the moment with an almost savage insistence, "I said to myself, This one is mine."

I will take you away from all this, I silently promise, horrified at what I am hearing. *You and Shelby both. I will rescue you. We will have us one of those instant families, like you see on TV.*

CHAPTER TWELVE

"There is no way I am not getting high for this dinner," I warn Gerald. "You want to go on the roof?"

"It's still light," he points out.

That is true. I do not usually indulge this early, but the thought of what is about to take place downstairs fills me with apprehension. Plus, I have not told him about my inviting Delilah, yet.

"Then we'll just do it in here."

"She might not like that."

"I think we are allowed to do what we want in the privacy of our own home."

"Not our home," he reminds me. "Hers."

"So she used that line on you too, huh?"

"It might be awkward if he smells it. John is faculty advisor to the school's Zero Tolerance Club."

"John?"

He looks at me.

"You know. Him."

"You mean Coach Kip."

"Nobody calls him that. I mean, we don't. He's going to be our stepdad."

I roll a joint and very pointedly close the window.

"Is it your intention to make a train wreck of this evening?"

"No!" I am offended. "Why would I do that to Mother?"

"I can think of a few reasons."

"I'm very happy for her."

I take an enormous first hit, trying to avoid Gerald's stare.

"He's not half bad, you know."

"That's hardly a ringing endorsement."

"You should see his penis."

I cough so hard he has to come around and pat me on the back.

"What is it about this guy's . . . *thing* that makes it such a topic of conversation?"

"It's just a distinguishing feature, that's all. You got to remember, I was on the team, his first year here. You were already gone. He changed along with us once. After practice."

"Apparently it made quite an impression."

"Big around as a beer can." Gerald shakes his head and hands me back the joint. "He's an OK guy."

"What are you going to do?"

"Long term?"

"Long term, short term, what are you going to do when she sells the house and moves into some kind of love nest with Mr. Budweiser down there?"

"I don't know. I have several things going on at once now."

"So I've noticed."

"What about you?" he counters. "How's your summer going?"

I shake my head.

"You're causing quite a stir, you know. Asking questions. Making scenes."

"Making scenes? I don't make scenes. I've been on my best behavior."

"—down at the auditorium, that night. Saying how we're all still slaveholders."

"Oh, that," I giggle. "Just speaking the truth. Besides, it was meant to be a compliment. I was defending the South."

"The South don't need defending. That's when you insult it. When you defend it."

Ever since he was old enough to have a personality, it was the right one, a way of meeting the world I recognize as infinitely preferable to mine. Nonconfrontational, yet getting what he wanted. People take to Gerald. For no reason. The same way they do not take to me, before I even open my mouth. He can be quiet and it is a positive reinforcement of whatever is going on, whereas when I stay silent everyone takes it as implied criticism. You would think I hate him for this, but of course I do not. He is my little brother. I feel responsible for him. It is a responsibility that, all through growing up, was barely a burden at all. Now, however, I sense he is coming up on a decision in his life, which is a rarity, that time when you consciously *choose*.

"Women only want one thing," I counsel.

"That's men, Kara. Men only want one thing."

"No. You should know this. Women only want one thing. *Everything*. So either one, if you're thinking of picking between them, is going to want all of you. And you have to decide in each case just what kind of Gerald they have built up in their mind. Because that's the one you're going to end up becoming."

"I have no idea what you're talking about."

"I'm talking about Delilah and the Mormon girl."

"Those are two different parts of my life. They don't necessarily have to meet."

"But they do meet. In you."

"That's a little deep for me."

I shrug. The gap, between even the closest of people, is almost always insurmountable.

"How about you?" he asks. "What do you want?"

I take the question seriously and, after a moment, admit:

"No clue."

"Glad we got that settled."

The doorbell rings.

"This probably wasn't a good idea," he says, stubbing out the joint.

"Are you kidding? It was totally necessary. Now we're going to have a great time."

He precedes me down the stairs. I remember, too late, what I wanted to tell him.

"It's from a vineyard in Chile," Delilah is explaining to Mother. "The man at the store recommended it. Can you believe they grow grapes there? I would have thought it was too cold."

She gives Gerald, who has stopped in mid-step, a kiss.

"Chile isn't necessarily chilly," I explain.

"What?"

"It wasn't named Chile because it was— Never mind."

I had forgotten her unique talent for turning *other* people's sentences into gibberish.

She is dressed (the result of much deliberation, no doubt) like a whorish nun, in a black-and-white ensemble that does not show any skin but manages to be almost sheer just the same. A lot of frills but no actual fabric, is the impression it makes. I can see it does not meet with Mother's approval, although what would? Maybe if she showed up in a pine box.

"Kara dear, will you help me in the kitchen for a moment?"

Her tight smile returns, reinforced by a garden-claw grip on my upper arm.

"Hey, that hurts."

In the guise of ushering me along, she tries dislocating my shoulder on the door frame.

"Be careful, you almost—"

"Did you invite that little tart over here tonight?"

"Tart? She's not a tart. I'm surprised to hear you use a word like that."

"Because I'm sure Gerald wouldn't be foolish enough to do such a thing."

"She's a perfectly fine person. What's the matter? You don't think she's good enough for him?"

"The table is only set for four."

"I'll be happy to lay another setting."

The doorbell sounds again.

"You go out there and mingle," I tell her.

"I'm not sure there's enough food."

"There'll be plenty of food. And look, she brought wine. She's a nice girl. I've totally come around on her. 'Tart,'" I chastise. "I could tell you about tarts. Some of the mean-ass bitches I've run into up North."

She looks at me.

"Are you all right, Kara?"

"Me?"

"You've been puffing away on that stuff again, haven't you? I can't believe you would do that on such an important occasion."

"Important occasion? It's not exactly Christmas or nothing. I mean, we're not expecting Santa Claus."

"Well! Well! Well!" Coach's voice booms.

"I'll fix the table settings," I promise, seeing her dire look. "Everything will go fine. You'll see. I think you're suffering from Hostess Panic. You'll get over it once the party starts rolling."

. . . probably *not* a good idea to get high, I amend my answer to Gerald, as she goes back out.

181

The knives, I notice, adjusting the utensils, seem unnaturally sharp.

Coach, not to be outdone, has brought two bottles of wine. They sit on the table, along with Delilah's, all untasted, three high-shouldered soldiers from some vermilion army. I try expressing that thought, or image, rather, but don't seem to make myself clear. Or perhaps everyone is so agog at my flight of poetic fancy that they do not know how to respond.

"Well, would you like some?" he asks.

"Sure. Why not?"

I do not usually drink. I am no longer on medications, but I was never that big a fan of alcohol. It makes me feel all muzzy and reduced. Under the circumstances, though, that might not be such a bad thing, I rationalize, accepting a glass, considering how all my previous sallies have been met with silence.

"John was born in Michigan," Mother resumes, "but he played his football at the University of Georgia."

"The Peach State," Delilah astutely comments.

"Ever since then I've led a kind of gypsy life."

"I used to cheer," Delilah says.

"Is that how you two met?" he asks, looking from her to Gerald. "On the sideline?"

She blushes.

"We weren't really that aware of each other, in school."

"I was aware of you," Gerald says gallantly.

"He was biding his time," Coach smiles.

"How did you meet?" Mother asks.

It is a moment, since she has not acknowledged them as a couple up until now.

Neither wants to say. They both begin speaking. Then stop.

"I'll tell it," Gerald says.

I take a sip. The wine is good, though, like almost all wine, would taste better mixed with 7 Up.

"A man came to the parlor and wanted roses up and down his arm. He wanted them on that thing, what's that kind of checkerboard you make out of wood so they can climb?"

"A trellis," Mother says.

"Right. A trellis, up and down his arm, with red roses. I told him I'd have to work on the design, that he'd have to come back. Then I went online and found some pictures, but they weren't exactly what I was looking for so I started walking around, looking at various people's gardens. I found one, up on Mayweather Road, a whole wall like that. A trellis. So I went to sketch it. I guess I should have asked permission, but I didn't think I was that close. I wasn't really on the property, just off to the side. So I took out my sketchbook and I was making a design when this big old pit bull came out. Those things move fast. I didn't have time to gather my stuff or anything before he was right on top of me, growling, baring those teeth of his. Then, out of nowhere, Miss Samson here appeared. She saw it all. She ran up and—"

He makes a gesture, sticks out his forearm like it is the crash bar of a metal door.

"—gets between me and the dog, I don't know how. That sucker sinks his teeth right in. He was a monster. I didn't know what to do. She wasn't making a sound though. And a second later, there's this CRACK!"

He is silent, letting the tension build. I drink the rest of my wine at one gulp.

"What happened?" I finally ask.

"I read it somewhere," Delilah offers, embarrassed. "'What to Do if You Are Attacked by a Pit Bull.'"

"Where do you read a thing like that?"

"I don't remember. *Us* magazine, maybe? Anyway, I just happened by and saw this dog coming up on Gerald. He didn't notice a thing. He was too busy sketching. So I ran over and did it. I didn't even think about it. There was no time. It was more like some kind of memory took over."

"Did what?" Mother wants to know specifically.

"You have to give them your arm." She demonstrates, holding it horizontally in front of her chest. "That's the hard part. Let 'em get into it good."

"—sank his teeth right in." Gerald shakes his head admiringly.

"But once they've got it, they can't let go. They can't unlock their jaw. So then you put your other arm behind their head."

She does that too, very stiffly. It is somewhat reminiscent of a cheer.

". . . and push *up* with your first arm, the one that's being bit."

"You broke his neck!" Coach exclaims.

"They can't let go, see? So you keep pushing, until you hear a sound. Until you feel something give."

"Broke his neck," Mother repeats.

"Then I took her to the emergency room," Gerald picks up the story, "over in Hot Springs. She had to get twenty-three stitches. Plus a bunch of rabies shots."

They look at each other.

"What about the dog?" I ask.

"Left him there," she says negligently. "He weren't going to bother nobody."

There is a different kind of silence, after the story. You can hear the almost mechanical sound we all make, recalibrating our opinions of this girl, mentally checking the condition of our own tender spinal cords, in case we ever get in her way.

"This sure is tasty," she chews, oblivious. "What is it?"

"Chicken salad." Mother stares at Gerald. "Why didn't you tell me about this, when it happened?"

"No reason," he shrugs. "Didn't want to alarm you."

"How'd the tattoo go?" I ask. "Of the roses?"

"Real good. That got me a lot of business actually. He was a member of a biker gang. Sent some more people over. That's when Delilah started hanging around the shop."

He smiles down at his lap, but whether it is out of newfound appreciation or the bittersweet memory of better times, I cannot tell.

"Jerr is so good at what he does," Delilah sighs. "I think I will try some of that wine now."

From then on, the dinner goes much better. Conversation becomes general. I try to prove I was raised right, not contradicting, not pontificating, not "showing off," as Mother used to call it.

"And what's this about a trip I hear?" Coach asks, pouring me another glass.

"Me?"

"You said something about that when we ran into each other downtown. Said you might be going on a side trip before heading up North."

"Oh, I was just talking."

"You're not driving back, are you?" Mother asks.

"I might."

I am having trouble juggling various truths in my head, trying to make them part of a coherent narrative.

"Drive what?" she frowns.

"I don't know. Maybe I'll pick up a car secondhand, here. Some old rent-a-wreck."

"And drive it to New York City? What would be the point of that?"

"Well, to stop off somewhere along the way, like I said to . . . John here."

"Stop off where?" she persists.

"Shreveport."

185

I just say it. Or maybe it says itself. This little molecule of a word. We all stare at it.

"Shreveport's nice," Delilah nods. "The whole ArkLaTex area."

"What's in Shreveport?" Gerald frowns. "That's not even in the right direction."

"You know."

I level my gaze at him. It's funny, the truth. How it wants out. How it needs to breathe.

He puts down his fork and pushes his plate.

"I didn't find out because of you," I add hastily, picturing Delilah snapping my neck like a breadstick. "I had a friend in Brooklyn do some research. He has access to all kinds of genealogical databases."

He is looking not to me, but beyond, to Mother.

"What's in Shreveport?" Coach echoes.

"Well, there's the Air Force Museum," Delilah lists. "Mardi Gras, of course. And the Red River Revels. But that doesn't take place until October, I think."

"Family," I answer. Gerald, Mother, and I have all pushed our plates away. "Most of my late father's relatives seem to be from around there. I imagine it's where he grew up."

"Kara," Mother breathes.

"I don't know why you didn't just tell me. Why you made me jump through so many hoops." I try to regain my composure, and turn to Coach. "I need a bone marrow transplant to guarantee my cancer won't come back. So far, I haven't been able to find any matches among my immediate family. There are people in Shreveport who might be able to provide me with some stem cells. Who might be able to *save my life.*"

"—shouldn't be going there," Gerald mumbles, barely audible.

"Why not?" I thump the table. Delilah is regarding me as if I have grown a second head, or maybe a third, considering how she looks

186

at me normally. "You two care more about *propriety*, about our good family name, than helping me get the best medical treatment. That's what it boils down to, doesn't it? No doubt I'll find some shameful scandal when I begin sniffing around Daddy's family in Shreveport. Maybe we got a touch of the tar brush or maybe his mom and dad were cousins. I don't know and I don't care! All I want is—"

"—don't need to go there," Gerald says again, in a strangled whisper. "You won't find any matches. It won't help."

"How do you know?"

"I just know."

"What your brother is trying to say," Mother awkwardly reaches across the table and takes my hand, "is that those people in Shreveport are not your blood relations."

"Yes, they are. I got me a whole family tree that says so."

"They are Gerald's family," she says. "His kin. Not yours."

"Well, how's that possible? How can they be Gerald's and not mine?"

I appeal to Delilah and Coach, our unwilling audience, as if to say, Look what a bunch of dodos I have to deal with. They are both regarding me, though, with the same queer expression. Even Coach, usually the one so puzzled, has a condescending, pitying stare.

"They're Gerald's family but not mine," I repeat. "How could that be? That could only be possible if—"

Mother is making a strange sound. Strange only because I have never heard it issue from her before. It is a soft, steady weeping.

"Jeannie!"

He gets up and comes around to her. She withdraws her hand from mine and buries her face in his belly.

"Well . . . *hell*," I say.

*

The dessert, the homemade strawberry shortcake she labored over, must be getting soggy. It is ridiculous to think of food at a time like this, but I did not have much to eat before the chicken salad hit the fan, so to speak. Downstairs, I can hear them cleaning up, Gerald and Mother. The clatter of plates, the dining room table leaf being removed, finally the thrum of the dishwasher starting up. I lie in bed, on top of the covers. It is too early to go to sleep.

"Kara?"

She pokes her head in.

"Who?" I ask.

"I thought you might be hungry."

"Who?"

Nevertheless, I take the dish, with its biscuit, fruit, and whipped cream. At least she can no longer tell me not to eat in bed. In fact, she can no longer tell me not to do anything, ever again. That should be liberating, but instead what I feel is crestfallen, that no one, anymore, is the boss of me.

"Who?"

"Stop acting like an owl," she snaps. "I heard you the first time."

"Aren't you having any?"

"I don't have much of an appetite."

"It's good."

"I'm glad."

She sits at the foot of the bed and smooths her apron.

"Do you macerate the berries?"

"Do I what?"

"Do you let the berries sit in sugar first? They taste sweeter than if you—"

"Oh, stop talking about the goddamned dessert."

"Well, I'm not allowed to ask about the other thing."

She takes a deep breath.

"He was not from around here. He was only here briefly. I was a very foolish eighteen-year-old, and it just happened. Neither of us intended it, and by the time I realized how far along I was he had moved on. I didn't even know how to get in touch with him. So . . ."

"So . . . what?"

"I left home, to have the baby elsewhere. There was a place my parents found, in New Orleans, for girls in my condition. About that time, I met your father. I mean, Gerald's father."

"Septimus."

"No, that was yours. I tried not to lie to you, Kara. I omitted a lot, but I tried not to lie."

"Gerald's known, this whole time?"

"Not the whole time, but for a while, yes. He had the right."

"And I didn't?"

"I didn't want to hurt you. And I didn't want to hurt your relationship with Gerald."

"What relationship? He's this half-ass stranger I spent my whole life thinking was my brother."

"I would slap you for that, but it would get strawberry juice on the quilt."

Instead, she does the opposite. She takes my sock-clad foot and begins stroking it. Tears are running down my face. I keep stolidly shoveling in the shortcake. It collects in my throat.

"So you knew about Shreveport."

"Of course. But I also knew it wouldn't help. Stanley was a good man. He loved you like you were his own. You would never have known, if this cancer business hadn't come up."

I manage to swallow, and then say, for the umpteenth and hopefully last time:

"I need to know my father's name so I can—"

"You don't think I looked? You don't think the *minute* I found out I started researching? You don't think I wouldn't do anything to save my beautiful baby girl?"

"No. I know you would. That's why it hurt so much, when you acted like you wouldn't."

"I thought I could spare you this, on top of all the other heartache you were going through. I looked. I found out. He was already an older man when I met him. He passed away fifteen years ago. He left no children. He had no brothers or sisters either. I confirmed that, both by state records and with the archdiocese."

"The archdiocese? How would they know?"

"He was a priest, honey. He was our priest. That's part of why I didn't want you to find out."

"A priest? You got to be kidding me."

"It was a very poor decision on both our parts."

"I'll say! How did—?"

"I don't want to get into specifics. It's still a very painful memory, after all these years."

"Well, what was he like? Can you at least tell me that?"

She pauses.

"He was the most brilliant man I ever met."

"And he left no survivors?" I ask numbly.

"You."

"I mean besides me."

"You're welcome to see my correspondence on the subject. I kept copies. I went all the way to the archbishop of Oklahoma City for information."

"What was his name?"

"James. Monsignor James Shepherd."

It takes a minute. I, too, do not want to get strawberry juice on the quilt. It is a very nice quilt. I set the bowl aside. Then I begin to laugh.

"I suppose I deserve all the scorn you are about to heap upon me," she says.

She's a *Shepherd*! Not a shepherd. A Shepherd! That is me. That is who I am.

I laugh more and more, realizing what all this means. It is certain now. I am going to die.

CHAPTER THIRTEEN

The parallels are too exact to be parallels. It is more as if my life is overlaid on hers. If it even is my life, not some childhood game. Let's play House. Let's play Get Taken Advantage of by an Older Man and Be Stuck with the Consequences. In her case, me. In my case . . .

I look around my room the next morning, the crumbling husk from which I emerged, flapped my wings, and whirred off to lead a brief mayfly life that turned out to contain no free will at all, to be as preprogrammed as that of any other insect. Mate and die.

Except you could not even get the mate part right, a voice taunts, as I feel my reassuringly flat tummy.

Where does this leave me? Of what use is my beloved Philosophy now? I am exactly the same as I was, yet every reference point in the world has been wiped clean away. I do not even know how to put my feet on the floor.

Some repressed celibate priest, thinking, late in the day, that he "loved" a girl parishioner. She is smart, serious, and asks him questions. Stimulates him. Makes him feel young again. I feel a perverse sympathy for the abuser.

But I hate that word, *abuse*. It is clumsy and clunky and sounds as if it is covering something up, the fact that she—the fact that I—wanted it just as much as him. Not the sex but the attention, the validation, the brief sensation of power that comes with being desired, especially when that desire is illicit.

"What do you want?" Gerald had asked, earlier yesterday evening, when he was still my brother.

Not to tool off to Shreveport in Christy Lee's fancy car. Not to resume my studies with the would-be father of my aborted child. And certainly not to stay here, in a position I am beginning to see as increasingly awkward, if not downright humiliating. How many people know? "She's a Shepherd!" If that gross old butcher man did, there must be others. Did the whole town? Have they all been snickering at me my entire life? Is that what made Mother so high-strung and proper and protective? On the other hand, look what I got in return, a whole beakerful of some obviously high-class DNA, top-grade stuff, not what you would normally find in this place's birdbath-sized gene pool. I straighten up a bit, try and hold my head high, while still stretched out under the bedding.

What do I want? I am awfully good at the negatives, what I do not want, whom I cannot be, where I will not go, but a positive template to replace the one shattered by last night's tawdry revelation, still eludes me.

The doorbell rings.

It is eleven o'clock. Mother and Gerald are gone, tactfully ceding the house to me, their half-bastardette-stepsister-product-of-unholy-incest. I yank open the door and surprise an acne-scarred youth.

Why is he so uncomfortable? I wonder. He rang the bell. He knew someone was likely to answer. Why does he nervously avert

194

his eyes and start reading off a pad held shakily in one hand? His other arm is awkwardly wrapped around a big box.

"Good morning, ma'am. I am looking for Mr. Karl Bell."

"Karl Bell? Who's that?"

"Mr. Karl Bell," he explains, as if repeating the name imparts more meaning, then shows me his handwriting on a stub, a whole pad of them, with their other halves ripped off. "He bought a raffle ticket from me on Spirit Day."

"I did that. I'm Kara Bell. You must have written down Karl."

"Oh." He examines the letters. "Well, our records show that you won."

"I won the raffle?"

"If you are Karl Bell of 22 Bluebelle Road."

"Yes, I am. I mean, close enough. Wait, I remember now. It was a speedboat, wasn't it? Did I win a speedboat?"

"No, ma'am. That was the Grand Prize. You won one of these."

He reaches into his box and comes out with a cup. One of many.

"What's that?"

"It's a thermal mug." He displays it proudly, as if it is *doing* something, besides violating my aesthetic sensibilities with its Witch's Falls Screaming Eagle. "It keeps cold things cold and hot things hot. You're one of our fifty honorable mention winners."

"Lucky me."

"You'll make sure Mr. Bell gets that, won't you?"

"I sure will."

He consults his mangled pad and goes off, lugging the big box like a traveling salesman with his samples.

Mother has left the coffee on. I pour a cup in my new thermal mug. It occurs to me that this may be the first thing I have ever won. I have been awarded scholarships and prizes, but to have something randomly bestowed upon me, out of the blue, is different.

Too bad it is not a speedboat, though.

I close my eyes and imagine heading for open water.

"I understand the deceased was a butcher. A cutter of meat."

The reverend, who at least has the decency not to pretend he knew Mr. Robbins, looks out over the mourners as if we should take a moment to reflect. This is made somewhat silly by there being just the two of us, Miss Pitts and me.

"A cutter of meat," he repeats. "Not a pretty job, but a necessary one, in our community."

In fact not, I object, remembering Ilene saying how everyone just goes to the Walmart now. Her floral tribute is here, from the Merchants Association.

He goes on to spin a rather tangled yarn about us taking each other for granted; how only through acknowledging our interconnectedness can we etc., etc. He is black, which is unusual—there are no mixed congregations here—and young, with a very carefully tended mustache. He tones down the Bible waving, either for our white benefit or because we are such a minuscule and unresponsive crowd.

"Mr. Robbins, from what I understand, did not attend regularly," he explains, when I ask about it, after. "Reverend Settles over at First Baptist didn't know him at all and had a previous obligation, so he requested I substitute."

"Professional courtesy."

"Something like that."

"You did a very good job," Miss Pitts adds. "You caught the essence of the man."

We watch the coffin be centered over the hole and then cranked down. There is no solemnity about it. There should be. A whole life, a cacophony of dreams and hopes and choices and acts. Grieving. Loving. Yet all I can picture is him pissing his pants.

A representative from the funeral home stands by the hearse. The reverend goes over to consult with him, or maybe get his check.

Miss Pitts hooks her arm through mine.

"I'm sorry," I say, "for your loss."

"It's nothing, really."

"You must have been to more than a few of these."

"Sometimes it feels like every other day."

"Are they always this small?"

"Often. People outlive their contemporaries, and their families, in John's case."

"At least he had you."

"And you." She squeezes me, not in a creepy way. Or perhaps I am over that. She seems less a person unaware of her desires than just another fellow creature in need. "It was good of you to come."

"I felt I owed it to him."

We watch them extract the equipment. There is a mound of dirt off to the side, but no one seems in a hurry to start shoveling it on top. Then I notice, lurking just beyond the cemetery proper, one of those small bulldozers. So that is what they will use, once we are gone.

"I can't imagine what you owed John Robbins. He was hardly one of our more sympathetic guests."

"He was trying to tell me something. Something I needed to know. But I was too dense to pick up on it."

Miss Pitts giggles. She is all in black. It suits her. She looks much better than usual. It is also the way she holds herself. She is more relaxed, not warring with her body, not such a mass of tics and grimaces.

"You've got to remember that Mr. Robbins's mind wasn't really *there*, toward the end. Whatever he told you, or tried to tell you, I think you should take with a large grain of salt."

"No. It was accurate, what he said. It just came out kind of funny."

"And calling yourself 'dense,'" she remonstrates. "Don't you ever say that. Why, you're a genius. You're worth ten or fifteen John Robbins."

"I'm not worth more than anybody else. None of us is." I can feel her getting all stiff, as if I have unintentionally offended her. "He was trying to tell me about my past, about my mother, and all I did was—"

"He was a liar! Everything he said was a lie. He was a mean dirty old man. You saw what he did to his drawers. On purpose! So some female would have to give him a sponge bath."

She shudders.

"All right, all right." I disengage my arm. "I didn't mean to get you all riled up."

"I'm sorry." She blows her nose with a much-used handkerchief. "It's just that if I'd known you already knew, then I wouldn't have . . ."

"Known that I knew what?"

"I'm not saying," she answers slyly.

"About Monsignor Shepherd?"

She looks around, though obviously no one is here. We are in a graveyard. The reverend is still giving us space. The workers have gone away. It must look like we are saying our final good-byes.

"So you know," she confirms.

"I found out last night."

"Damn!"

I am surprised to hear her curse, on hallowed ground, or surprised that it strikes me as so wrong.

"Well, ain't that a kick in the pants?" she says. "And here I went to such trouble."

"What trouble? What do you mean?"

"I heard him, in his evil, roundabout, nasty way, trying to tell you about Jean. About the trouble she got in."

"So you knew too?"

"Of course I knew. But I would never say. It was horrible, what happened. It was a sin, on many multiple levels. And no one would have expected it from your mother. She was such a quiet girl. John Robbins, I could tell, even with his brain tissue mostly holes, that he was trying to upset you, trying to ruin your time here. That's why I put him down. But if I'd known you were going to find out anyway I probably would have let nature run its course."

"Put him down."

"Well, you know." She nods to the hole. "Some people need a little help, getting over that final hump. That's part of the job. I ease them. Ease them across. To Jordan."

"Are we done?" the reverend asks, coming back.

"I think so."

Miss Pitts gives him a warm smile.

She seems almost sexually satisfied. She has a cat-like purr to her voice and a lazy grace to her movements.

"You mean you've done it before?" I whisper.

"Believe me, dear, it was always with good cause. You don't know what I have seen, in terms of suffering."

"No."

"Now Mr. Robbins here, he was more a case of the suffering he caused in others, but still, I promise you, what I did was right and just."

There certainly is no doubt in her mind. She turns to survey the stones with a certain amount of pride.

"You remember that story I told you about my mother taking me on an Easter egg hunt? How I couldn't bring myself to stoop down and pick up a single piece of candy? Well, sometimes I think *this* is my field, and what I am doing is stocking it, kind of the opposite of what was expected of me. I am laying down all the treats, making this world a better place for the children of the future, one person at a time."

199

I do not know what to say. My mind, unwilling to deal with the central fact, loses itself in speculation on the details. Did she inject them with poison or use a pillow or offer them a specially doctored can of her precious Coca-Cola Classic?

"That money you lent me, I'll pay it back as soon as I can."

"No worries," she says gaily. "That's how they speak in Australia. I heard it last week on a TV program. 'No worries.' It's my new motto."

"It's a good one."

"You want to get something to eat? I must confess, funerals always make me hungry."

I'll bet. I picture her munching away on a bacon strip while selecting her next victim.

"No." I hesitate. "There is someone here I have to visit."

She nods knowingly and puts her hand on my shoulder.

"You don't let any of this upset you, hear? Your job is to persevere."

"Yes ma'am."

"I do wish you could call me Justine."

"All right, Justine. Thank you, for everything."

"Oh, it was no bother," she says, looking back over the freshly dug grave.

I wait until she is out of sight and then go to my father. Or whoever he was. Leaving, we each used to put a pebble on top of his stone. The three of us. They would get blown away or washed off by the next time we came. Hundreds of them are scattered in the surrounding grass. I sit so we face each other. I would like to say something, but since I never knew him, and now know him even less, if such a thing is possible, words utterly fail. A man who briefly loved me, though even in that brevity he is still the current world-record holder.

Certainty, the certain health, the certain future, I had hoped to find by arriving at Truth, where is that?

A man clears his throat. It is the reverend again. I thought he was long gone.

"Am I interrupting?"

"No. I was just having a little sit-down, here."

"Don't get up. I'll join you."

He sets himself down next to me. I look at him sidewise. He cannot be more than thirty.

"My father," I say, as if introducing.

He nods.

"Must be tough, giving the eulogy when you don't know the man. I guess you have a couple of one-size-fits-all bits you can resort to."

"Albert asked me to pass along a message, if I saw you."

"Albert?"

He takes a pebble and puts it on the stone.

"Oh. A.C! But how'd you know it was me?"

"He described you."

"In graphic terms, no doubt. You're not from around here, are you?"

"Kansas City."

"How is A.C.? I mean, Albert?"

"Fine. That's the core of what he wanted me to say. That he's doing well. He felt he left you a little worried, the way he was talking. Things are much better now, he says."

"Sounds like you don't believe him."

"I want to believe him. But naturally, I'm concerned."

"Naturally."

"And what about you, Miss Bell? Are things better for you?"

"I wasn't aware they were ever bad."

"He had mentioned that you were dealing with some health issues."

"Did he? Albert tends to dramatize."

He smiles. He is putting a whole row of pebbles across my father's—across Stanley Bell's stone, spacing them like they are the knobs on fancy fence posts.

"I miss him," he says.

"Wait a minute. Are you Lonmell?"

"Reverend Richardson."

"Right." I look him over again. I can almost hear A.C. going, "Uh-huh," like he used to when we drove by a basketball game. All those sweaty shirtless bodies. "Just what was it that made A.C. take off that way? Do you know?"

"I know some of it."

"He wouldn't tell me nothing."

"I think he felt you had enough on your mind."

He finishes ornamenting the stone. When I come back, they will all be gone. But now I realize I never will come back. There is no reason to.

"I've been meaning to go to the Bait Shop," I say. "Check in on Mae. She must be lonely, with both her men gone."

"Don't you know? The Bait Shop's closed. Mae's left Witch's Falls, as well. Nobody knows where."

"But not with A.C.?"

"No. Not with Albert."

"What happened?"

"Seems there was some kind of stuff going on down there, illegal activity, and it all came to a head. They took off in various directions, the three of them."

"But they're a family."

He nods, as if to say that is not out of the question, such things happening, that families sometimes cease to exist.

"I was close to them, growing up. Or thought so," I go on moodily. "I guess they weren't that close to me, though."

"Albert was."

"You think?"

"He tends to push away those he cares about."

"Don't we all?"

"I certainly hope not."

I try looking into the man's eyes but they are guarded. There seems to be pain in there. And answers, I am sure. But I have no right to pry. The very things A.C. was protecting me from, he will protect me from as well. Yet I would like to do him a good turn.

"So Albert is the one you're in touch with."

"More like he's in touch with me. When he wants."

"He'll want," I assure him. "You're his soul mate."

CHAPTER FOURTEEN

"The Battle of Poison Spring had to do mostly with corn," Martin explains. "The Union Army was starved for resources and sent out several wagons to raid the Confederate stockpile at White Oak Creek. Upon their return, they were confronted by units under the command General John S. Marmaduke. A spirited battle ensued, during which the Union forces were driven into a swamp, forced to abandon their ill-gotten gains, and suffered heavy casualties. It was one of the most decisive Confederate victories of the war . . . in this state. That is what we commemorate here today."

I am, as was promised, in gray, although only a common infantryman. Martin has some rather elaborate braided gold rope working, as well as a hat that would not look out of place on the cover of *Vogue*. He, I read in the accompanying handout, is General Marmaduke himself. Ilene, standing beside him in the back of the flatbed truck that has delivered weapons, bottled water, and small pieces of artillery, looks more like a member of some modern-day militia in a patterned pants suit of updated Confederate camouflage. But the best-dressed prize goes to Shelby, who wears a heartbreakingly cute baby version of Martin's historically accurate general's uniform, though with different markings, I notice.

"Who's Shelby supposed to be?" I call, from down in the rabble surrounding the truck.

"Shelby!" she answers, holding him up high for us to see.

Several people applaud.

Of course. General Joseph Orville Shelby. "The Undefeated." His namesake.

I am issued a cheap plastic replica of a vintage rifle.

"Any bullets in it?" I ask hopefully.

"Are you kidding?" the man handing them out grunts. "It don't even fire."

"Kara?"

I turn around to find Candy, the girl behind the counter at Kreski's. She too is a foot soldier.

"I see here we're Company B," she says. "You and me."

"We're going to win this war single-handed," I promise.

"What?"

"How come there's no bayonets on these things?"

The arms distributor eyes me.

"Don't get much call for bayonets."

"We're supposed to report to Sector D," Candy announces, scrutinizing the map.

"Let's get going."

We are a few miles outside of town, in the state park. I know the terrain, even though the names on the map have been changed to reflect an area south of here. How typical, I think, as we trudge along, that Martin has picked what sounds like some minor skirmish with no bearing on the outcome of the war itself, only because it is a rare "success," and is local.

"How's things at the luncheonette?"

"What?" she repeats.

It seems to be her knee-jerk response, when confronted with

any question. She is a slow, suspicious type, on the meaty side, with tiny eyes.

"How long have you been at Kreski's?"

"I think we're supposed to talk historical."

"What, like in character?"

"Well, isn't that the point?"

"I don't know." I hadn't really considered. "You mean like it's 1864?"

"Yes."

"And we're guys?"

"Well, not *that* historical."

She detours around an invisible rock, to put a little more distance between us. In your dreams, sweetheart, I feel like telling her.

"All right." I think for a moment. "How's things at the luncheonette?"

"Never mind."

"Well, don't you think they had luncheonettes back in 1864? Where else did they eat?"

"I don't know."

"What do you want to talk about instead? Robert E. Lee?"

"People say you got a baby taken care of. Is that true?"

Now it is my turn to stumble on an invisible stone.

"I suppose things like that took place in 1864, too," I admit. "And it is probably just what two transvestite soldiers would discuss on their way into battle."

"Did you?" she persists.

"Why? Are you going to refuse me service at the counter now?"

She is carrying her rifle in a very unprofessional manner, dragging the barrel along the ground.

"Oh." I look again. Meaty, yes. With unwanted child. How blind I have been. "I can tell you where I went, if you're interested. I can give you all kinds of numbers and information."

"Too late," she says disconsolately. "Besides, I don't think I could go through with it."

"It's not nothing, but it's not the end of the world. It's like you are admitting Error into your life."

"Which?" she asks. "Having it or not having it?"

"I don't know. Both. Neither. I don't know nothing, really."

. . . which, for me, is quite an admission. But I can see I am not doing her much good.

"Going to be OK either way." I give her a hearty slap on the back, as I have seen army buddies do. "The important thing is to defeat the enemy."

"You're weird."

"I'm a rebel. You are too."

Sector D turns out to be a small hill overlooking an interior road. Our flag is planted there, the Stars and Bars. We are instructed to lie in wait, ambush a company of fleeing, cowardly Yankees, and slaughter them, I assume, without mercy. Our commander (a foreman at the processing plant, Candy whispers) shows how, by pushing a concealed button near the trigger, you can make the rifle produce flashes of light and bursts of noise.

"So it's nothing more than a child's toy. Why don't we get to use real weapons?"

"There have been incidents," he says darkly.

"A foreman in real life just happens to be a sergeant in the army," I note, after he leaves. "Martin Casimir, the richest man in town, is the self-appointed general. And we, who are nothing, are assigned the role of cannon fodder. You beginning to see the paradigm here?"

"I'm not nothing."

"Neither am I. But we are treated as such."

"You're talking insubordination."

We settle down in our spot surveying the road.

"So whose child is it, if you don't mind my asking?"

"None of your business."

"He going to make it right? The man?"

"He can't make it right."

She sniffs, snorting up tears. I want to be sympathetic, show my solidarity, but do not know how.

"They got no justification," I say angrily, "coming here, telling us what to do."

I am speaking of the Union soldiers (more correctly called "Federalist" if you believe in the cause, if you want to link it up to today's secessionist–Tea Party–Klan movement) but I mean for it also to apply to men, and the rich, and pretty much anyone who gets in our way, all those who stray within the sights of our battery-powered "for ages five to eleven" guns.

"The thing is," she says, "I don't think he knows."

"Doesn't know it's his?"

"There's a kind of disconnect."

I am surprised to hear her use such a modern word.

"I mean, he knows what we did. And he knows what I am, my condition. But he doesn't seem to add the two things up."

"So what are you going to do?"

She shrugs.

It is as eloquent a gesture as any I have ever seen. Wittgenstein built the most amazing system for understanding—or rather for refusing to understand, obviating the need to understand—the world. It is remarkably constructed and completely unassailable. Its very nature precludes objection. Yet, years later, a colleague made him doubt much of it by making a wordless motion of brushing his chin, a clearly articulated statement that had no place, could not fit, in his exquisitely modeled universe.

The best answer to such a shrug is an equally silent acknowledgment. I settle into the kind of pose I have seen in war movies and

TV shows, stretched out, belly-down on the ground, rifle trained, one eye closed, the other squinting.

The sun is hot. The somnolence of this part of the world works its way into my bones. I allow my mind to loose itself from its moorings and drift, recalling the primitive, propulsionless creature it evolved from. I may even sleep, though it feels like I am awake. I sense I am getting at something, some idea in my head, perhaps even beginning to think critically and creatively again, after such a long hiatus, when a thug plants his boot squarely on my back.

"In the name of the Union Army, I declare you prisoners of war!"

We both look up, or try to. The light is in our eyes. When I finally manage to sit, I see four people from town, wearing blue, looking embarrassed, holding our same Mickey Mouse firearms, led by an older man in drab olive, a real army uniform with all kinds of battle ribbons and what looks like, secure in its holster, an actual pistol.

"Major Green?" I blink.

"Hello, Kara." He briefly becomes the kindly man who would offer me a ride home from the library in his enormous Lincoln Town Car. Then he frowns again. "I'm afraid you ladies are POWs, now."

"What?" Candy asks.

"But we can't. We're supposed to wait here and ambush these Union forces that are coming down that road."

"That would be us. Corporal, confiscate their weapons."

A man I recognize as the owner of the shoe store snatches away our mock rifles.

"We circled around behind you," Major Green boasts. "That flag you got flying was a dead giveaway."

"But that's not fair."

"Apparently this is what happened, according to the historical record. I've got my orders right here."

"You mean we were set up?"

"You're not even wearing the right clothes," Candy notices.

"I was given special permission. As a retired military man, I didn't feel it proper to don another uniform."

Or maybe you lost your Union Army outfit drawing to an inside straight against some poker-playing prostitute, I think, remembering Mother's explanation of why the Major no longer believes in salvation.

"Corporal Allen here will escort you ladies to the holding area for those who have been declared captured."

"And that's it? It's over? The battle?"

"It is for you. Maybe next time you'll have better luck in your assignment."

"Well, screw this," I mutter, as we watch him and the other blue shirts go off.

"They might've told us," Candy complains.

"If they had, we wouldn't have agreed to it."

"Where's this holding area?" she asks our captor.

"About two miles down that way."

"Two miles!" she wails.

"The highway's right there," I say. "Just over that rise. If we don't have any more part to play in this farce then we could just go there and hitchhike home."

"You can't do that. You got to return your uniform and weapon."

"You've got my weapon," I point out. "And I can always hand in the uniform later."

"Let's go." He changes his tone, pointing us down the road with his rifle.

"He's right," Candy sighs. She does not have an ounce of gumption in her. "We got to do what he says. We're prisoners, now."

"The hell we are. Come on, Candy."

I walk off in the other direction. I can hear cars beyond the last stand of trees.

"Stop that," he calls. "Halt."

"Oh, for crying out loud, it's just a game. Besides, don't you think plenty of rebels ran off rather than be captured?"

. . . especially by a shoe salesman, I add silently, or maybe not so silently. It has evolved into a surprisingly tense moment.

"Kara," Candy says uncertainly.

"Come *on*," I try urging her to follow.

"I'm warning you."

He levels his rifle.

"You'll never take me alive!" I shout.

The sounds are remarkably realistic. I cannot vouch for the flashes, as my back is turned, but I instinctively zigzag down the road as if real bullets are whizzing by. Such is the power of mass delusion. Panting, I stagger into the woods, hide behind a tree, and peer around the trunk. He is not in pursuit. He has given up on me and settled for Candy, who resembles nothing so much as a cow being trooped off to slaughter.

I think about giving a hooting, wolf-pack yell of freedom, as my ancestors were wont to do, but instead just yawn. Soldiering is hard work.

At the road, I am presented with the exact same dilemma I faced during college graduation. Since I finished high school early, I had never participated in one of these events, and did not realize that you were supposed to wear regular garments under your cap and gown. When the rental company demanded their return almost as soon as I stepped off the makeshift stage, I had nothing else on. It is even worse with the Johnny Reb outfit, since I cannot ask a family member to run back to my room for a change of clothes. Instead, I present to the world my usual trick-or-treat spectacle, thumbing my way along Route 10 looking like a sweaty extra from *Gone With the Wind*. Some people honk appreciatively, or derisively, but no one stops. Finally, a Land Rover comes bouncing out from the park. Martin is at the wheel, still in his safari hat.

"Kara, they told me you got lost."

"I didn't get lost. I escaped. I'm on my way home."

"No record of any escapees," he pronounces, amused.

"That's quite a set of wheels you got."

"Isn't it? Little present to myself. Hop in."

I do not need to be asked twice, it being several hundred degrees.

"How could you do that?" I grouse, letting the wind that is generated as he resumes driving penetrate my baked wool. "Allowing those guys to sneak up on us from behind."

"You had a very significant role to play. You were part of a feinting maneuver. In order to appreciate the reenactment, you have to look at the big picture."

"You're not returning me to that concentration camp, are you?"

"No. And it's a holding area. This is not the Holocaust. Just a little exercise in civics."

"What do you care anyway? I mean, your Polish ancestors, no offense, couldn't have found this place on a map in 1864."

"But they were farming dirt then, just like the folks around here. Not that big a difference."

"Where are we going?"

"—said you wanted to get back to town, didn't you?"

"Yes, but don't you have a war to run?"

"Won't take more than a few minutes."

I lean back. I have spent time with Martin, but only in the company of Christy, or watching his public persona at the school auditorium and when he addressed the assembled armies from the bed of the truck. It is not clear to me if we have anything to say to each other.

"I didn't mean to cause such a fuss."

"All part of the plan," he shouts back.

There is no roof, just a roll bar. On the highway it is loud but also refreshing, the naked speed.

"What exactly is part of the plan, my freaking out?"

"That, and my happening upon you. Whatever occurs, I always figure it's for a reason."

"Can I ask you something? You really care about the Battle of Poison Spring?"

"I care about the name recognition it gives me. Very noncontroversial name recognition, which is the best kind. There's a state senate seat opening up in two years. Might come in handy, people knowing who I am."

"Another little present to yourself?"

"I'm not saying, one way or the other. How's your cancer?"

That is the good side of Martin, I guess. He is so rich, so aristocratic, if you can talk about an aristocracy in such a rustic backwater, that he can afford to ignore the niceties, the social pussyfooting that makes most talk here like eating cotton candy.

"Hard to say. I feel recovered from the chemo and radiation. I haven't had any more spells. Now it's just this horrible waiting. I have to go on up to New York for all kinds of tests, and then keep getting tested every six months, to see if it comes back."

"What are your chances?"

"There's no way of knowing. There's numbers, but they don't tell much of a story, really. I just have to figure how to live with it. The possibility."

He nods, digesting that, not offering sympathy, for which I am deeply grateful.

"But how do you feel right now?"

"Fine," I answer automatically, then cancel that. "Different."

"Different how?"

"Not in control."

He takes us off at the exit but does not proceed into town. The Rover is cool. It gives the impression you can go anywhere, that paved roads are just society's suggestions, to be avoided rather than confined to. There is a never-used picnic area and, off that, one of the many two-gulley dirt paths that meander through the backwoods, a whole network from earlier times, connecting farmsteads that no longer exist. I hold on to the steel frame. He brings us to a stop under the shade of an oak.

"In school," he says, removing his hat, "you impressed me as the kind of girl who was always in control, no matter what."

"You must've needed glasses," I joke. "Back then I was a certified nut."

"And now?"

"Less so," I admit, with something like regret. "I wonder, I know it's superstition basically, but I wonder if all the treatments, and maybe the sickness itself, have robbed me of whatever specialness I had."

"I doubt that very much."

"It seems to have taken away my ability to reason."

"You mean to study philosophy?"

"You don't study philosophy. You do it. That's what we say. 'Do philosophy.' It's a very important distinction."

He puts his hand up my shirt.

As I said, there is nothing underneath. Who knew it was another graduation? When I got to where we were all assembled, I immediately saw everyone else had a layer of street clothes. It gave me the familiar feeling of not fitting in, of not understanding the simplest thing.

"Stop that. What are you doing?"

"What I've always wanted to."

He has turned to fully face me now, in his uniform, which has all kinds of elaborate bric-a-brac on it. He clearly outranks me.

"Is this how you plan to run for senate?"

"Pressing the flesh," he grins.

"No."

I stop him, though all that does is clamp his palm over my breast. There is something comic about it. A tremendous misunderstanding.

"I know," he says, reading my mind. "I know, I know, and I know."

He is ticking off the objections, one by one, even before I have managed to formulate them.

"But," he concludes, "I want to."

"Why?"

He shakes his head. That is the less appealing side of the upper-class approach. Never bother to question.

"Well, I don't."

I squirm out of his grasp and try climbing from the car. But he blocks me. Not in any kind of aggressive way, just shifting his weight so I am pinned against the seat back.

"I never pictured you as the rapist type."

"I never had to be. Never encountered much in the way of resistance."

"Well, this is what it feels like."

"That uniform suits you."

"No, it doesn't."

"Why don't you let me be the judge of that?"

"Martin." I try channeling his mother, figuring that is probably the one woman he listens to. "I am your wife's best friend. Plus, I don't *do* this."

"Always with your nose in a book," he reminisces dreamily. "For some reason, I found that incredibly attractive."

"It wasn't meant to be. It was meant to be the opposite."

"And now here you are, a little soldier boy."

Something pokes me. Something really sharp. I scream.

We both look down.

It is a ceremonial sword. I had not noticed him wearing it on the back of the truck. It is so tailor-made, the scabbard and handle, that it fits right in, melds with the rest of his uniform, all the gold trim and jangling medals. That is a hard thing to carry off, fashion-wise, a sword, but Martin has managed to do it, up until now. It does not really go with forcing yourself on someone in the back of a Land Rover, though.

"You mind getting rid of that thing?"

He unbuckles the belt and lets it fall to the floor of the car. I take the opportunity to jump out.

"You sure?" he confirms, watching me, not at all abashed, safe from within his customized rich man's domain.

"It's a kind offer."

"My father liked to read."

"So I've heard."

"He had a whole roomful of books. They're mine now. I thought maybe you could help me read them."

"Ah, the misunderstood businessman."

"Don't want to be understood, by most people."

He gives me a look, not one I am used to receiving. If I were not already red-faced, I would blush.

"I wouldn't mind being understood by you."

"—not sure I'm *that* smart."

He grins.

"Don't you want to go back and win the war, Martin?"

"It's a foregone conclusion," he shrugs.

"Well, that's where we differ. My fate still hangs in the balance."

He repositions himself, then revs the engine and takes off. I hold my breath until the fumes dissipate, look down and see my knees shaking, knocking against each other.

Martin Casimir. I try replaying all our previous encounters, going back to the third grade. Except there are none. He simply does not exist for me, except in relation to Christy.

Stop trembling, I order my legs.

Obediently, they do.

Christy though, now that my mind has come upon her, refuses to let me go. I happen to be quite near her part of town. This stone wall, amid the scrub pine and overly ambitious bushes, is the same that borders her backyard. It is a seam running through the landscape, gray boulders and gray-green lichen, randomly heaped but that randomness following a deep order. They lead somewhere, the stones. They demarcate something. The edge of what was once a vast field, or the border of a large farm, a plantation even.

I smile and shake my head. He did not know what he was doing. He did not know he was giving me permission.

"Little soldier boy, my ass," I answer, striking out across the wilderness.

He thinks I am no longer in play, as he drives back to his make-believe world of swords and state senate seats. But he has, in fact, untied me from myself. I quicken my pace, not a soldier anymore but a deserter, outside the rules. I feel sexually reckless, the way I was supposed to feel at sixteen but never did. Perhaps it is the sun. Or perhaps it is the still disgusting feel of his fingerprints on my chest. I want to expunge that, do away with those oily marks. For once, I have a very clear idea of where I need to go and what I need to do.

CHAPTER FIFTEEN

From behind, the house looks vulnerable. No great porticoed door or wraparound porch. No plantings tended by a service that comes once a week to mow the lawn. Just Shelby's wading pool, playpen, and a few deck chairs. But Shelby is not here, I remind myself. Neither is Ilene. Or Martin.

I emerge from the woods. Of course she could be gone. I cannot see if the car is out front. But as I take a few more steps, I enter her magnetic field, feel its pull.

Oh, won't you give this poor parched runaway something to drink?

Why, I couldn't possibly refuse, she will say, frightened for her safety, turning, leaving the door slightly ajar.

In fact, the sliding screen has been left pulled all the way open. I step into the kitchen and pause, listening for any kind of sound. There is a creaking, directly overhead. The master bedroom, where she took me that first night. I kick off my shoes and mount the stairs, grateful for the thick pile, for my toughened soles. I am dry-mouthed. My heart is pounding.

No more thought, I resolve.

Nevertheless, I am not bold enough, at the end of the hall, to do more than knock. There is no response, but I know she is there. I can smell her. Not perfume. Her. I knock harder.

"All right," she mumbles, sleepy, sullen.

I step back from the door.

She is in a robe. A terry-cloth robe, loosely knotted. She takes one look at me and bursts out laughing.

"Goodness gracious! You look like you been through the wars."

"I have," I answer, though it comes out more a croak.

"What are you doing here? Are you lost?"

She is overwhelmingly beautiful. Overwhelming me, certainly. It is because she did not intend to be seen, is just woken, without any kind of face to confront the world. There is a nakedness to her, even to her robe, hastily thrown on, the way the knot of the belt is slowly, casually working its way undone.

"—came to see you," I say.

"Do tell."

"No. I mean, I think this was all about coming to see you. From the start."

"I'm flattered."

She puts her arm up against the door frame, effectively barring my entrance, yet at the same time freeing more of that sleepy warmth which is just about the sorest temptation I have ever encountered.

Why, I argue, regard it as temptation? Why not regard it as encouragement?

"Whoa. Slow down, soldier."

I have her in my arms, though I do not remember traveling the last six inches between us. It is a lost blip in time.

"I ran away."

"No, you didn't. You went to college. That was good. I envied you."

"I mean just now. I ran away."

"Oh. You ducked out on Martin's little game?"

"Don't talk about him."

"He must've been ticked off."

"I knew you'd be alone."

"Kara." She grabs the hair on the back of my head, it has grown long enough to do that now, and yanks it, hard, to stop my clumsy attempt at locating every square inch of her exposed skin. "Not sure if I like you this way."

"Sure you do. Shelby's there. I saw him. Ilene too. They're all gone."

"You're sweet."

She is still holding me back, just by the hair, but that is enough to stay my entire body. It is how she communicates, by violating personal space. She looks me up and down.

"Let me in," I say. Then I manage to hit that note I know she likes, of false bravado. Self-deprecating. Half joking. "You won't regret it."

. . . though this time I mean every word.

Her laughter is of a different kind than before. The grip her fingers have on my scalp softens.

"Who *are* you?" she asks, noticing my uniform.

I reach past her and push the door. Her robe is nearly the softest thing on Earth, second only to what lies underneath. I walk her, we are dancing, a few steps backward into the room. Someone is crying on the big bed.

"I mean, I appreciate it that you've finally gotten some color sense, in your clothing, but I can't believe you let them make you a nobody. A common soldier." She investigates the markings, or lack thereof. "I told Martin you should be a colonel, at least."

The girl is naked, what I can see of her, past Christy's shoulder, with the sheet drawn up in a show of primitive shame. There is an expression of terror on her face and her eyes—I have never seen

221

anything like it—are not coordinated or focused. Her pupils are huge and off center. They roam frantically in deep sockets, trying to escape.

"It never rains but it pours," she sighs. "I believe you two know each other."

"No."

She frowns.

I look again.

It is Amy, the missionary. Without her dark glasses.

"No need to have a conniption," she calls, not bothering to turn. "It's just Kara. You remember her. From that park we went to, in Little Rock?"

Her response is a yelp, a torn wail of grief.

"Oh, for pity's sake. Excuse me."

She readjusts her robe on her way to the bed, belts it tighter. I watch her sit and comfort the child, whispering and stroking her side. It quiets her, instantly.

"I apologize."

She means for the unpleasant spectacle.

"What—? How—?"

She fights the urge to laugh again.

"You should see your face. No, no, dear. I wasn't talking to you." She continues to absentmindedly soothe her. "Amy here has been instructing me in the finer points of the Mormon religion. Or the Church of Latter-Day Saints. That's what they prefer it to be called. Haven't you, dear?"

"Stop," I say.

"I do not recall inviting you to break into my house today, so please stop looking at me like I am the Wicked Witch of the West."

"What did you do to her?"

"Nothing! Am I not allowed to have a moment?" Exasperated,

she gets up, shrugs out of her robe, and starts to dress. As if I do not exist. "Everyone else around here seems to get one."

"Get what?"

"Moments of true feeling. That's what Miss Amy and I were trying to have. What we *had*," she corrects herself. "Though now, as you can see, she's ruining it by getting all guilty. I don't know why. She certainly seemed to be enjoying herself. Why are you having all these second thoughts?"

"Maybe religious scruples?" I suggest.

She has turned from us and curled into a ball, her body heaving with inaudible sobs.

"This is the part you like best," I tell Christy. "The damage."

"You think?"

She honestly considers the accusation, appraising the wretched, regretful form as if admiring her handiwork.

"I just don't know," she concludes, as much to herself as me. "I trust my instincts. I mean, what else do you have to go by? But sometimes they lead me astray."

"You're going to have to drive her home."

"What a drag. That is not going to be a thrill ride, for sure. You want to come?"

I shake my head.

"You're much more fun than she is."

"Shh."

"Oh, she doesn't get offended. She's grateful. Aren't you?" She goes over and speaks right into Amy's ear as if she is deaf, as well. "Because now you know what's what. Believe me, you're going to sleep better tonight."

"Stop, Christy."

"You are going to wake up tomorrow and thank me."

"I got to go."

"No, no. Stay."

She has thrown on jeans and a shirt. I wish I could say that I suddenly see her for what she truly is, but, in fact, she has never been more attractive. The only new element is her need. Her fear of being left alone.

"Come downstairs. I'll make us a drink."

"It's not even noon."

"It's five o'clock somewhere. I'm sorry. I didn't mean for you to see this. It's just an unfortunate coincidence. You're supposed to be out there with the others. I thought I had me a day."

"I got to go," I repeat. "Besides, you have company."

"Yeah." She rolls her eyes. "Do you know that Mormons don't just mate for life, they mate for all eternity?"

"I did not know that."

"That paints a pretty grim picture, don't it? I know more about Joseph Smith than I am ever likely to forget."

"I'll bet she could say the same about your ass."

She claps her hands in delight.

"That's the Kara I miss. Come on. Come on downstairs with me."

"No."

I back up until I am out of the room.

"It was just something to DO!" she screams. "It is so fucking boring around here!"

I close the door, close the door on the scene, is how it feels. One that will continue to play out, after I depart.

At the bottom of the stairs, I think of what I should have said: "You married well."

. . . because it is true. They are two peas in a pod, her and Martin.

I walk home through the empty streets. Everyone is still at the event. So am I, in my mind. I am the allegorical depiction of Defeat, a disarmed, disillusioned private, on her way back to a world that no longer exists. Passing by a house, I hear music. Or not music, notes, rather, played very fast. They stop, repeat, and stop again. Over and over. It is someone playing exercises, strengthening her technique. I like the sound of it, how it goes nowhere and is *hard*. Difficulty. There is a concept I have not run across in a while. Difficulty for its own sake. The challenge.

I go up to the window from which the notes are coming. There is a flower bed. I carefully place my feet on the in-between bits of empty earth. Shading my eyes, I see Corinne, immersed in her playing, her bare feet, with that painted piano on their toenails, pressing the pedals, her fingers feeling, flying, tripping sometimes, but then picking themselves up, as they traverse the keyboard. I stay a few minutes, watching and listening. It is like seeing back in time, the concentration of adolescence, to the exclusion of all else; that exclusion being, of course, just as important as what she is focusing on, as if by a sheer act of will she could stop, for one last precious moment, the world from flooding in.

"Is it going to hurt?"

"Well, there's a whole debate about that."

Gerald has a good manner, like a doctor who can give a shot without you even noticing. He goes about his business, never changing speed.

"Some people say it hurts, later. They remember it hurting, but at the time . . . I guess they're just expecting it to be so much worse, gritting their teeth and clenching their fist, that they're kind of surprised when I tell them it's done. Others, they make it a point of honor to say that they never felt a thing."

"I guess it's all in the mind."

"Women are better than men."

"At what?"

"Pain."

It is night. The parlor is closed. We are in back, just the two of us, in a circle of bright white light. My arm is flexed out on a table next to the chair. The electric needle waits alongside, creating a small operating theater.

"This is a somewhat sensitive area," he cautions, positioning my forearm so the pale underside faces up. "Back, shoulder, ankle all have less nerves."

"I want to be able to see it."

"There's always that consideration."

"Which is better, if I watch or look away?"

"—up to you."

I decide to look at the shadowy corner of ceiling and wall. There is nothing there, which makes it more possible to penetrate with my gaze. The needle starts. It is less dentist's drill than sewing machine. I try not to hear.

"So she just up and left without giving notice or anything?"

"They said she was no longer assigned to the Outreach Center. That's all they'd tell me. Then I went and found the girl she roomed with. According to her, she decided to go back to Salt Lake City from one day to the next. No explanation."

"That's odd."

"Doesn't matter, really." He changes slightly how my arm is lying. He is holding me down. "I had pretty much decided not to go through with it."

"Really? Why?"

"Turns out they don't like tattoos."

"No."

"Funny, but it never came up. Because she couldn't see, I guess. I mean, they don't make you take off what you got, but they frown on you getting any more."

"So you could have kept yours."

"That's not the point. It's what I do. I'd still be putting them on. It would be hypocritical. Besides . . ." His voice goes a little sheepish, which is endearing, "it's my art."

"You tell 'em, Gerald," I encourage, trying to delve deep into the cobwebbed corner.

"No one to tell," he reminds me, hurt.

Was it love? I wonder. Unconsummated, impossible, crazy, spiritual love?

"So what are you going to do?"

"Go to San Diego, I guess."

"San Diego?"

"They got a wild scene there. Lots of military. Delilah's been checking it out online. She even sent some of my work to places. Got a couple of responses."

"Good weather," I say vaguely.

That is all I really know about the place.

"How about you? What are you going to do with your share?"

It has all happened so fast. Coach concluded his "custardy" battle, which allowed Mother and him to become a more public couple. Then he got offered a job at a junior college in Lexington, Kentucky. They are moving before the start of the fall semester, living in sin, thank god, as I am not yet ready to contemplate being a maid of honor. (Ironically, it is Mother, not Gerald, who is converting.) The house, which she sold in a day and a half, went for more than expected. In an act of generosity, she is giving us each a third.

"No clue," I frown.

"You said that before."

In a way, the money is a distraction. It represents all this potential—places to go, time to fritter away—but there is no one thing I want.

"I have a question for you, Gerald."

"Shoot."

"I asked before where you saw this wave and you said it was just in your head."

"Mmm?"

He is working away. There is pain, yes, but it is so regular and predictable that my mind can anticipate and, to some extent, neutralize it. Besides, the pain itself is not . . . painful. Not after the initial surprise. It puts my senses on high alert, sharpens them. I am *aware*, even if it is an awareness of damage being done.

"But when you told that story about doing the tattoo of roses, you said you went looking for a model, something in real life to copy from. Ow!"

"Sorry." He pauses a moment, then resumes.

"So what about with this wave? You've never been to the ocean, have you?"

"I been to the Gulf."

"That's what everyone around here says. The Gulf of Mexico is not an ocean."

"Surf-cam," he says matter-of-factly. "They're set up in all the surfing hotspots around the world. So you can see what the weather's doing, what the waves are like, at any given time. I don't remember which one this is from."

"Thank you."

"What difference does it make?"

"I like to know the answer to things."

"The answer. But you got 'no clue' what you're going to do," he reminds me. "What's the answer to that?"

"What I'd like . . ." I let my eyes travel beyond where the walls and ceiling meet. My mind too. "I'd like to go to the beach where this wave is from, and sit there, and do absolutely nothing. Just watch the water pound the sand. Have the sun burn every thought out of my head. Forget who I am, for a while."

"Pardon me for saying so, but isn't that pretty much what you've been doing this whole summer? I mean, not with waves or anything but basically you've just been *being* here, right? You told me yourself you didn't get any work done on your PhD thing."

"So you're saying my tattoo is more about remembering?"

"That's what most of them are. After all, you can't really ink in a picture of the future."

He works in silence.

"You're still my sister, right?"

"Of course."

"Good. Because there's no charge for family members."

In the Saint Louis airport, I watch people load up on calories at the fast food concessions.

We had to throw out a ton of stuff, getting the house ready. Mother was appalled that I did not want to take anything with me.

"We could rent a storage unit."

"Where? Here? Lexington? New York City?"

In the end, we used a truck and took a whole load of stuff to the dump, which explains why I am traveling light, with nothing more personal than a Screaming Eagles thermal mug.

"Why on earth are you taking that?" she asked.

"Because I won it."

I have several hours. And then a life after. Or not. I have already contacted Saul. He knows I am returning to start work on my dissertation. He also knows we are resuming our relationship on a different footing, one more conducive to my long-term goals. I stretch out my arm so I can admire Gerald's work. The swelling has gone down. It provides a spiritual exercise. Now, when I feel things slipping away, I center myself right beneath the curl as if I am surfing. I make those crucial little movements on the board, tiny adjustments, midcourse corrections, to stay upright, all while rushing forward.

"That's beautiful," a woman says. "May I see?"

Can a voice alone be thrilling? I never considered the possibility. Yet this one is. It brushes against every thought I have and sets them all in motion. If history takes place in the future, that is where I am. I lift my gaze out of myself . . . and look over.